# Shadowland

*The Converse Court in the Great Library had acquired a new statue. A young man dressed in white and gold with a spiked silver mesh wound into his golden hair. He stood facing the central pulpit, one hand on the hilt of his sword and the other clenched in a fist, regarding the empty air before him with an expression of implacable rage.*

Kal, the Archon of Shattershard, has been put under a spell while trying to save Morgan from the sentence passed on her by the Converse Court, and now he is frozen, an immovable sculpture in an attitude of fury.

Morgan and Alex were condemned to return to Earth for ever and have left the Court under escort, accompanied by Ciren and Charm, two agents of the sinister faction of the Wheel—but will they reach their destination?

Zoe, left behind with Jhezra and the still-blind Laura, is afraid: afraid that Alex and Morgan are being led into a trap; and afraid for her own future and her companions' in the increasingly threatening world of the Library.

Rhiannon Lassiter was born in 1977. Her mother is also a writer and reviewed for several newspapers, ensuring that Rhiannon always had something to read. She began to read science fiction and fantasy when she was about nine years old and it is still her most enduring passion. She has always spent a lot of time reading and writing and even skipped classes at school to go to the library. The first novel she sent to a publisher wasn't accepted, but the positive feedback she received was a great boost to her confidence. Her first trilogy was published just after her nineteenth birthday, which meant combining her univer[illegible] degree with her writing. Rhiannon now lives in Oxf[illegible] friends and two cats. *Shadowland* is the [illegible]ries which also includes *Borde*[illegible]

Shadowland

Also in this series

*Borderland*
*Outland*

# Shadowland

Rhiannon Lassiter

OXFORD
UNIVERSITY PRESS

Great Clarendon Street, Oxford OX2 6DP

Oxford University Press is a department of the University of Oxford.
It furthers the University's objective of excellence in research, scholarship,
and education by publishing worldwide in

Oxford New York

Auckland Cape Town Dar es Salaam Hong Kong Karachi
Kuala Lumpur Madrid Melbourne Mexico City Nairobi
New Delhi Shanghai Taipei Toronto

With offices in

Argentina Austria Brazil Chile Czech Republic France Greece
Guatemala Hungary Italy Japan South Korea Poland Portugal
Singapore Switzerland Thailand Turkey Ukraine Vietnam



First published 2005



British Library Cataloguing in Publication Data

Data available

ISBN 0 19 275239 1

1 3 5 7 9 10 8 6 4 2

Typeset by Palimpsest Book Production Limited, Polmont, Stirlingshire

Printed in Great Britain by Cox and Wyman Ltd, Berkshire

**Dedicated to Chris Fox**

Because writing inside books is like
taking things out of their boxes.

# Prelude

The Converse Court in the Great Library had acquired a new statue. A young man dressed in white and gold with a spiked silver mesh wound into his golden hair. He stood facing the central pulpit, one hand on the hilt of his sword and the other clenched into a fist, regarding the empty air before him with an expression of implacable rage.

In all the known worlds the Great Library is a thing apart. Inhabited solely by agents of the mysterious organization known as the Collegiate, it is said that even they do not know its true purposes or extent. Beyond this plain room lie hundreds of thousands more; all with the same book-lined walls, the same unassuming wooden furniture, the same open archways leading through more shelved corridors to more book-filled rooms. Papered with books and riddled with Doors, magical portals to other worlds, the Great Library holds more secrets than a lifetime of study could encompass.

In the Converse Court a group of people had clustered around the frozen figure and were murmuring softly to each other as they studied it. The young man's motionless body was covered with a dazzling haze of silver sparks, which fizzed violently when one of the surrounding people came too close.

'It looks like a spell,' someone was saying as a young woman, wearing a curved sword and a sickle-shaped dagger, came to join the edge of the circle.

'Dalandran cast a spell on him earlier but it should have worn off now,' one of the Jurists replied. 'He was a trial witness who had to be suppressed.'

The newcomer had been listening to this with only half an ear, studying the motionless figure with a troubled look, but now her brown eyes flashed and she spoke for the first time.

'His name is Kal khi Kalanthé and he protested when this court separated him from his lover.' She glanced around the circle with a fierce glare to fix her gaze on the last person to speak. 'You said the spell should not have lasted so long. Seek the magician who cast it and bring him here. Now.'

The Jurist she spoke to blinked in surprise but, taking in the dangerous look in her eyes and her confident stance, swallowed the objection he had been about to make and nodded instead. The other bystanders edged away a bit and then backed up further when the young woman turned towards them, finally melting back into the rest of the crowd that wandered through the room. As they did so, a younger girl with a mass of reddish-brown hair came up beside the fighter and stared into the dazzling haze that surrounded Kal.

'What's going on, Jhezra?' she asked.

'I don't know.' The dark-haired girl frowned. 'One of the Jurists said the spell that was cast should not have lasted this long.' She paused. 'What do you think, Zoë?'

'It looks like static electricity,' Zoë said thoughtfully and then shrugged at Jhezra's look of incomprehension. 'A kind of energy.'

Slowly she put out a hand towards the figure and then suddenly pulled it back. Jhezra looked at her with sudden concern but Zoë shook her head, looking embarrassed.

'I'm fine,' she said. 'It was just a nervous reaction. Static electricity gives you a shock . . . a jolt if you touch it. I'm a bit scared to touch him.'

'I could . . .' Jhezra began but just then a tall imposing figure in dark robes strode up next to them and said in clipped tones, 'Did one of you want to see me?'

It was Dalandran, the magician who had sentenced them. Jhezra turned towards him but although her eyes were angry her voice was calm and controlled.

'This person came to you for justice and you cast a spell on him. Perhaps you would now remove it?'

'He was out of order when he objected to our verdict. Nonetheless, I'm gratified to see you've obeyed the court's order to set aside your blood feud with him,' Dalandran said sententiously and then looked towards Kal with a frown. 'Give me a moment,' he said and closed his eyes, assuming an air of concentration.

The two girls watched him silently for a moment and then Jhezra asked softly, 'Where's Laura?'

'I don't know and I don't care,' Zoë said bitterly. 'This latest mess is all her fault. I'd never have come to the Converse Court if I'd realized how this would end.'

'Speak softly,' Jhezra warned, taking Zoë's arm to move her away from the figure of the magician. 'But I agree.' She looked over at Kal's frozen figure and said, 'I believe the court tried to be just . . . but how could they know the full truth of what has happened to us?'

'Laura was very convincing,' Zoë admitted. 'But she used us all to get revenge.' Her expression faltered and she bit her lips unhappily and Jhezra remembered how young her friend was.

'It's not your fault,' she said, squeezing Zoë's arm in a gesture of reassurance.

'I just feel so responsible,' Zoë said miserably. 'Everywhere we go, everything we do . . . just makes things worse.' She looked at the floor and her voice trembled. 'I wish I'd never taken a step off Earth.'

'You could have gone back,' Jhezra said carefully. 'When the Jurists sent Morgan and Alex home.'

'Yeah, right.' Zoë's voice hardened as she looked up to meet Jhezra's eyes. 'If you believe for one minute that's where those Wheel agents are taking them . . . I wouldn't trust them as far as I could throw them.'

Jhezra couldn't help a bubble of laughter at the foreign expression, translated through her amulet. But her expression grew serious again immediately.

'You don't think they were telling the truth?' she asked and Zoë shook her head.

'Morgan and Kal didn't trust them,' she said. 'Even the Jurists weren't completely certain or they wouldn't have sent those two bodyguards along too. Plus they looked like robots or zombies.' She shuddered. 'Did you see their *eyes*?'

'I did,' Jhezra said grimly. 'And I agree.' Her gaze drifted back to the rage written across Kal's immobilized face. 'I don't think Kal will be pleased when he awakens.'

'If he wakes up at all,' Zoë said, looking miserable again. 'He's another person whose life we've destroyed.'

Jhezra tried to find some comforting words for Zoë.

The younger girl might feel guilty but Jhezra knew better. The devastation of her home world wasn't Zoë's fault; she of all of them had the least involvement, having been dragged into a situation she knew nothing about against her will. But then Dalandran turned away from Kal's motionless body and looked at them with a puzzled expression.

'This spell is none of my doing,' he said. 'It's a defensive magic that deflected my spell and now continues to hold this young man bound.' He shook his head. 'It's magic of a type unfamiliar to me.'

'Then you can't take it off him?' Zoë said, concerned, and the magician shook his head.

'No,' he said. 'I cannot.'

# 1

Alex Harrell, walking down a book-panelled corridor under guard by four Collegiate agents, was trying to work out how everything had gone so badly wrong.

He'd always prided himself on his logical mind. Back on Earth when he, his sister Laura, and her friend Morgan had first discovered the Door Between Worlds he'd taken a practical approach to everything. While Laura played politics with the merchant guild and Archon's court and Morgan had fallen in love with the idea of herself as a magician, Alex had done real things instead. He'd learnt to ride and fight and had come up with a workable plan to conquer the city. The city's destruction had been a terrible accident, one that had left him shell-shocked for a while.

Coming to the Great Library had been a bad mistake and seeking help from the Jurist faction a worse one when Morgan and Kal turned up and laid charges against them. Laura's testimony to the Court had dumped him right in it and she'd saved herself at his expense. While she'd been exonerated of any guilt, he'd been blamed for the destruction of the city of Shattershard and agents had been appointed to forcibly return him to Earth. It wasn't any consolation that his sister had done the same thing to Morgan.

Morgan had been taken aback when she was held responsible for cursing Laura with blindness. Either she honestly hadn't known about the rule against harming other world travellers or she thought it didn't apply. Alex could see how she'd come to use her magic against Laura and for a moment in the Converse Court he had thought she would do it again. But Laura had convincingly made Morgan look like a psychopath and now she stumbled along beside him with blank eyes, as if she still couldn't accept what had happened to her.

Back on Earth he'd only known her as his sister's friend, two years below him at school. In Shattershard she'd seemed pathetic, making people think she was a powerful mage because she wore black. Only recently had he come to realize that her magic was both real and dangerous. But now she seemed in the same dazed state he'd been in after the fall of Shattershard and the collapse of his hopes and dreams. Not like someone with a deadly and controlled magic but a victim going to the scaffold.

He couldn't expect any help from Morgan. It looked as if they were going to be taken back to Earth whether he liked it or not, since he was only one against four. The two who walked at the back of the group had spoken to each other quietly a couple of times but he hadn't been able to make out their conversation. The two at the front had walked in complete silence, setting the pace for the group and choosing the turns and twists of the route.

He was still trying to understand how all these Collegiate factions worked together. The agents at the back were Jurists, appointed by the court to see them safely to Earth. The ones at the front had described themselves as agents of the Wheel. They were eerily similar and although they looked like teenagers they had spoken like adults to the Court. They seemed to know everything about the Collegiate and how to cope with its arbitrary rules and obscure customs. They were dressed plainly and their pale pointed faces and weird dark eyes made them look meek and fragile. But Alex couldn't help looking at the weapons they wore: the wooden longbow slung over the boy's shoulders and the short swords hanging from the girl's belt.

Their names were Ciren and Charm and Morgan had been afraid of them. Alex wished she were alert enough for him to whisper to her and ask why. He suspected it had to do with magic. He'd never paid much attention to otherworld magicians and now he was suffering the consequences of that; having no idea what the twins were capable of.

'We are approaching the Bridge Across Darkness,' Ciren said aloud, turning to regard them with those strange black-purple eyes. 'We must watch where we walk.'

'What do you mean, the darkness?' asked one of the Jurists.

'See for yourself,' Charm said stepping aside, and looking past her Alex found himself suddenly blind.

The illusion passed as he looked back to the others and he blinked as he tried to make sense of what he was seeing. Underneath his feet the wooden floor continued as before and a row of hanging lights suspended from the low ceiling glowed dimly from above. But on either side of the passageway, where there would normally be the inevitable shelves lined with books, there was nothing. Instead of walls was a void of impenetrable blackness, as dark as the Doors Between Worlds.

The two Jurist agents took the lead on to the bridge, moving slowly and uncertainly. Ciren took Morgan's arm and guided her after them. With Charm gesturing that he should precede her, Alex had no choice but to obey.

As he stepped on to the bridge he was instantly claustrophobic. It wasn't that long since he'd been trapped beneath Shattershard, stumbling down narrow tunnels through the debris of fallen rock and seeing the path ahead dimly in the feeble light of Zoë's electric torch. Now there was wood just above his head and beneath his feet and the darkness on each side was like a wall.

To distract himself he squinted through the darkness, trying to work out what it was. Like the Doors Between Worlds it was totally black. At the edge of the corridor it cut off as cleanly as a cliff face. The first time he'd walked through the Door he'd fallen over, disoriented by the passage. It had only lasted an instant but the feeling of being enclosed so entirely in blackness had been like passing out. Staring into the darkness on the side of the bridge he wondered what would happen if he were to jump into it.

'It's been tried.' Charm's voice came levelly from behind him. 'No one came back.'

'There are other experiments.' This time Alex could hear his voice sounding unstable and he could almost feel the hairs rising at the back of his neck at the way Charm had effortlessly read his mind. 'You could tie someone to a rope . . .'

'They come back unconscious or raving.' Ciren's voice

floated back to him in measured tones as if they were having a pleasant conversation. 'Don't walk too close to the edge or you might faint and fall.'

'But why is this here anyway?' Alex asked, trying to keep control of his voice. 'You called it the Bridge Across Darkness.'

'There's a theory,' Ciren said, his voice the only sound in the black void that surrounded them, 'that the Library exists in the space between worlds and the Darkness is what remains when you take away the walls and the books.'

'Is this something your faction constructed?' one of the two Jurists asked from ahead but Charm didn't answer and Ciren was speaking to Morgan.

'See, we're nearly at the end of the passage,' he was saying and Alex stared past him to see an oblong of light outlined ahead of them. The darkness cut off around it like a television screen and Alex wrenched his eyes away as he realized he was feeling dizzy.

Behind Alex, Charm spoke suddenly, causing him to straighten up instinctively.

'The Bridge Across Darkness is on the way to the most closely guarded worlds of the Wheel. It is one of the methods we use to protect ourselves.'

Alex had stepped off the end of the bridge just before she spoke, into a small square book-lined room. He heard the sudden edge in her voice and flinched away in time to see the blade of a sword flash past him.

Flattening himself against the side of the room, Alex saw Ciren pull Morgan out of the way, turning her head so she wouldn't see what was happening. Charm's swords sliced through the air so fast they seemed to hum as she cut the first Jurist once across the face and twice across the stomach, rending flesh and spilling blood and entrails in a sticky mess. The man screamed and fell, dead before he hit the ground from the look of the blood pooling from his open throat.

'No. Please . . . Don't do this . . .' The second Jurist was backing away, whimpering under his breath as Charm stalked forward, her face expressionless save for that small smile.

The smell of blood hung heavily in the air, iron and tannic, and Alex seemed to see in slow motion the blood running down Charm's swords and dripping on to her hands as she raised them once more.

'Mercy!' The second Jurist's cry was lost in a bubbling sound as Charm slashed downwards. Blood spattered the floor and walls and across the rows of books that lined the room.

Charm turned to regard Alex with a small smile.

'But we have many ways of protecting ourselves,' she said, picking up the conversation as if nothing had happened.

Morgan whimpered and Alex caught a glimpse of green eyes wide in a pale face before Ciren drew her further away.

'Don't be afraid. The Jurists were your enemies, Morgan,' he said. 'They wanted to imprison you on your own world. We're your friends. We rescued you from them.'

Morgan didn't seem capable of response but Alex found himself replying, speaking unsteadily because the smell in the room was making him nauseous.

'They were sent to make sure you took us back safely to Earth,' he heard himself saying, hardly believing that he was arguing the point. 'Since you killed them you must be planning to take us somewhere else.'

'Do you object?' Charm's voice was cold but her lips were still set into the same sweet smile. 'Returning to

Earth was supposedly a punishment for you. The Jurists wanted you cut off from the Collegiate.'

'I want to know what's going on.' Alex's voice didn't tremble as he finally tore his gaze away from the red sheen on Charm's blades and met the doubled gaze of the twins. 'I thought you were on their side when you said you knew the way back to Earth, but you killed them. Are you seriously asking me to believe that you did it for Morgan's sake?'

'We don't ask you to believe anything,' Charm said. 'We work for the Wheel and we answer only to our patron.'

'So where are you taking us?' Alex asked, looking from one twin to the other. 'To this place of yours you have to . . . protect?'

'It's called Chalice,' Ciren said, speaking as much to Morgan as to him. 'It's very peaceful, very safe, and very beautiful.' His dark purple eyes met Morgan's compellingly. 'It's the world you've been looking for,' he said.

Alex watched doubtfully. It wasn't as if there was anything he could do about it or any reason why he should even care that the twins seemed to have Morgan spellbound. But in the circumstances he doubted everything they said.

'Nonetheless, it is what you're looking for,' Charm said and he turned with a start to see her watching him and smiling. 'Power and a weapon and a cause to work for.'

Alex was silent but Morgan's forehead creased as if she was trying to remember something.

'Is it your world?' she said uncertainly, looking towards Ciren. 'Is that where we're going?'

'It's the world of our patron,' Ciren told her and Charm stepped forward to move Alex along as she added,

'Chalice and everything on it belongs to Vespertine Chalcedony.'

Laura Harrell tied her green silk scarf, feeling its smoothness under her careful hands as she bound it across her blinded eyes. She'd only been blind for a couple of weeks but already it felt like forever. She couldn't imagine what it would have been like to be sightless back on Earth but, strangely enough, the blindness seemed to fit with the person she was here.

Laura imagined herself as others might see her. A girl with light brown hair and bandaged eyes, who held herself straight and tall despite her disability. A girl who had defended herself against accusations in the Jurist court and triumphed over her enemies. A girl who looked helpless in the face of weapons and magic but whose words had a power that could not be denied.

She smiled to herself, savouring the feeling of triumph. Laura had always known she had the power to rule worlds inside her and here, in the Great Library of the universe, she had found it.

'You must be very happy,' a voice said and Laura turned her head slightly in its direction.

'How so?' she asked. It was Glossali Intergrade, a young Collegiate man who had guided them through the Library and whose advice had helped her to manipulate the Jurists during the trial.

'You won!' Glossali said. 'They punished the girl who blinded you and sent her back to her own world . . . aren't you pleased?'

'I suppose so . . .' Laura said softly and her shoulders lifted and fell in a small sigh. 'But I'm still blind, Glossali . . . How can I survive like this?'

'No true Collegiate member would ever harm you,'

he said hastily, his words stumbling over each other in an effort to reassure her. 'Why don't you come and stay with my faction, the Catalogue Cult? We'd look after you . . .'

'Thank you, Glossali,' Laura said, turning her face towards him and trying a small brave smile. 'But I have to go on. I haven't given up hope of a cure, you see.'

'Oh, of course. I should have realized,' Glossali replied, and Laura felt his hand touch hers gently. 'But you can't just strike out all alone . . .' He radiated concern and she imagined his face flushed with worry for her. 'You're safe in the Great Library but there are savages out in the worlds. Anything could happen.'

'I know.' Laura suppressed a smile, thinking of everything that had happened already, and hid it by putting her face in her hands. 'I don't even know where to begin,' she said in a voice that trembled with laughter as she felt Glossali put an arm around her shaking shoulders. 'Tan Ecesis said my only hope was to find a world without any magic at all . . . because the spell on me wouldn't work there.'

'A world without magic.' Glossali thought about it and then said with renewed enthusiasm, 'There must be some. Your own world even . . .'

'No.' Laura jerked her head up sharply, a frown creasing her forehead. 'Not there. I'd be nothing there.' She hastily softened her voice as she turned towards Glossali again. 'I have to find a place where I can be useful, or I'll just be a burden to my friends.'

'You could never be that,' her supporter reassured her. 'But I understand your feelings.'

'So can I.'

Laura started and felt Glossali jump as well at the sound of a newcomer's voice. It was dry and held a hint of amusement and after a moment Laura placed it as belonging to Lisle Weft.

'I gather you're not content with the court's verdict, Laura Harrell,' the voice continued and Laura couldn't avoid the feeling that she had been seen through. Lisle Weft was an elderly woman, a member of the Jurist faction who had asked some penetrating questions during the trial. Laura wondered uneasily how much the woman had overheard of her conversation with Glossali.

Composing herself, Laura smoothed down her hair around the blindfold and replied, 'I was just telling Glossali that I have other ambitions besides achieving justice,' she said and to her chagrin Lisle laughed out loud.

'I'm sure you do,' she said. 'But I thought I should warn you that this might not be the place to pursue them.'

'Why not?' Laura asked suspiciously and there was a pause.

'I think perhaps this is a conversation best had in private,' the elderly woman said. 'Perhaps you might give us a few moments alone?'

'Oh certainly.' Laura heard Glossali move to leave before he thought to add, 'If that's all right with Laura.'

'Yes, go,' Laura said impatiently, frowning under her scarf. Glossali had been helpful so far but Lisle was by far the more interesting character since she obviously knew the Great Library well and her faction, the Jurists, were far more effective than the foolish Catalogue Cult. Although Laura had the impression that the woman disapproved of her, she couldn't help being intrigued.

The Great Library was not safe. Laura knew that even if Glossali did not. But she was ready to face the dangers when there was so much to gain. The Library Doors led to hundreds and thousands of worlds. She'd been a fool to waste her time trying to take over Shattershard when she could pick and choose from worlds without end.

According to the twins this new world was named Chalice. Alex didn't trust anything they said although he couldn't see what reason they would have to lie about it. But when Ciren and Charm had murdered two other Collegiate members in cold blood, he'd realized that trusting the twins was a way to get yourself killed.

Alex had been a warrior. Not for long; and his first serious battle had put an end to the war. But he knew something about killing, more than the other teenagers from Earth realized and he knew that if someone could kill so easily, without warning and without offering the possibility of surrender, you could never turn your back on them. So now, he wasn't thinking about escape or even attacking the twins, he was thinking about how to stay alive.

So far his prospects didn't look good. The twins had taken him with them so that they'd be believed when they promised to take him and Morgan back to Earth. But instead they'd killed the Jurist witnesses and brought Morgan here, as a tool for their faction to use, and the only reason Alex was still alive was that so far they hadn't thought it necessary to kill him. This was only the fourth world Alex had ever been on, not counting the Great Library, and he knew nothing about how it worked. But his new plan meant that he had to know everything that could help him to stay alive so he watched and listened and said nothing.

The Door had opened into a plain square of stone, bracketed at four corners with half-pillars; uniformed guards stood behind each semi-circle shielded by the stone and with weapons held ready. Even that told Alex that he had finally hit the big time.

This world was organized. The guards' uniforms had the same black and red insignia that stood for the Wheel. This was a world that the Wheel controlled and the only way to reach it was through a Library section they also controlled, or through Doors that would be guarded.

'Agents Ciren and Charm reporting in,' the boy twin said and the guards relaxed minutely while another soldier with extra flashes on his uniform saluted from the edge of the stone square.

'There are two bodies on this side of the Bridge Across Darkness,' Charm, the girl twin, said expressionlessly. 'Send a Sanitation Squad to retrieve and cremate them.'

'It will be done,' the commander said and made some kind of signal behind him. Alex didn't look to see where. His mind was feverishly trying to process all this information.

Ciren and Charm were young but they weren't only trusted agents, they gave commands and expected them to be obeyed. This commander might not be very senior but he was an adult and he was in charge of at least these four Door guards and probably a troop of others.

'Also arrange for increased guard duty at this position until further notice,' Ciren added and Alex thought it hardly seemed necessary.

This wasn't a world that people were getting on or off without the Wheel's permission. The commander saluted again and Ciren and Charm started walking, Ciren keeping his light hold on Morgan's arm. Morgan didn't even seem to notice she was under guard. She was crying again, the tears just spilling out of her eyes and leaving shiny snail-tracks down her face.

'This way,' Charm said to Alex and he started walking.

He could feel the eyes of the Door guards on his back as he walked. He forced himself to remember that the real danger came from the twins. It was they who would attack or, more likely, give the order to have him cut down.

Beyond the stone platform there were more stone buildings and a straight gravel path leading between them. The buildings were only a storey high but Alex could see that walkways and parapets linked them at the top and the corner positions were all guarded. The path they followed led through the centre of what Alex was certain was an army barracks and came out the other side, and suddenly Alex could see for miles.

The stone buildings were at the top of a hill. A hill so square and regular that it might be artificial. The path ahead widened into a road with a surface as smooth as a road back on Earth. Beyond the road was a countryside divided into squares. Fields were divided by low stone walls with roads running in between them. Smaller buildings were grouped at regular intervals and in the far distance fortified positions like the one they had just come from stood on more hills, regularly spaced about the landscape, extending as far as the eye could see to the horizon with the pale grey-violet sky.

'This is Chalice,' Ciren said again, his attention on Morgan, but Charm was already looking over to her right where another soldier snapped instantly to attention.

'Summon transport to Vespertine Chalcedony's villa,' she said. 'For three.' She turned to look at Alex with her lips twitched into a tiny smile and he felt his stomach turn over, certain he was about to hear the order that would have him killed.

'Vespertine may wish to question him,' Ciren said and Alex could only stare, not even certain that the words meant a reprieve until Charm looked away from him again.

'This is Alexander Harrell, an inexperienced and unallied world traveller with some understanding of the Collegiate. Schedule him for Salvage.'

'Yes, sir, right away,' the soldier said and he glanced at Alex for a second to add: 'You, follow me,' before turning crisply on his heel and walking away.

Now was the moment to say something if he wanted to stop the twins disposing of him like unwanted baggage or perhaps to say something to Morgan or make some gesture. But it was too late. All he really wanted was to get away from the twins and his body had already stumbled into motion at the order and he was following the soldier away.

'Mancer, Drake, have a transport here on the double,' the soldier snapped, throwing the words over his shoulder to two figures Alex barely glimpsed before they set off at a run.

He wetted his lips to try to speak to this soldier, anxious to know what Salvage was. But he was led at a military jog-trot back inside the barracks and, almost before he realized what was happening, ushered into a plain stone room.

'Stay here. Don't leave the room,' the soldier said and waited for a beat.

'Yes, yessir,' Alex managed to say and the man nodded and closed the door in his face.

Morgan watched Alex taken away and another part of her died inside. Once, years ago, she'd had something of a crush on Alex. During the excitement of discovering the Door Between Worlds it had melted away and she'd lost her awe of him. Now, she didn't even like him, but when he was gone she had lost her last link to the past.

Her face felt raw and numb simultaneously. Her mouth and nose stung and it was hard to breathe. It hurt to cry and hurt to stop and Morgan wondered if it would ever stop hurting. Around her people came and went, exchanging words with the twins, but she couldn't speak. Everything seemed to be happening on the other side of a veil as thin as gauze and as heavy as lead.

'This way,' Ciren said, his hand on her arm guiding her forward and upwards through the door of some kind of coach drawn by two grey horses. It was high, three steps off the ground, with slippery leather seats inside and small high windows with shutters.

Morgan slid across to the far side of the seat and against the side. In the darkness of the coach, pressed into the corner, she felt the tears start again.

'There's no need for distress,' Charm said, as she followed her twin into the coach and pulled the small oval door shut behind her. 'You've been rescued, remember?'

'I don't think she can hear you,' Ciren said. 'She's shell-shocked.'

'She can hear me,' Charm said. 'But her mind is like fog. She hears but she can't find words to speak.'

'Will Vespertine find that acceptable?' Ciren said, and Morgan felt a sense of resentment stir at how easily they discussed their plans while she sat next to them.

'Does it matter?' Charm was saying. 'We've achieved what we were sent to do.'

'No. It doesn't matter,' Ciren replied but then he fell silent himself.

The twins had been her friends. Before she'd found . . . but Morgan wouldn't think about Kal. She'd met

Ciren and Charm in the magical guild-house in Shattershard. They'd frightened her at first but when she'd got to know them she hadn't found their difference so strange. Morgan's friends had always been odd, the people on the edges of society who no one else could be bothered with.

Laura was the only friend she'd had who was popular, and that was because people on Earth didn't know Laura, didn't know how little she cared about anyone except herself. Zoë hadn't been her friend at all, caring too much about appearances to waste time on anyone not at the centre of things. If it hadn't been for the Door Between Worlds Zoë would never have spoken to her. Alex had never been interested in her, or in anything she found interesting, treating her like a child playing with toys while he concentrated on more serious business. Only one person had ever seen her for who she was.

Laura didn't know what to make of Lisle Weft. The older woman had helped them at first and then later sat in judgement over them but Laura had the impression that through all of it Lisle was thinking and feeling very different things from the public persona she presented. She was a politician, much more so than the other people they'd met in the Library, and Laura wondered uneasily if perhaps the older woman could read people as easily as she could herself.

Lisle travelled everywhere with a dog, although Laura only knew this because the others had told her so. Most of the time Pepper was quiet, only making a sound if Lisle herself seemed angry or upset. Now, trying to make a friendly gesture, Laura extended a hand towards the floor.

'Is Pepper with you?' she asked.

'Naturally,' Lisle said calmly. 'Perhaps you should consider some form of animal companion, to guide you.'

'Perhaps,' Laura said vaguely. She'd never had a pet; her mother always claimed dogs and cats brought in dirt and she hadn't been able to find the idea of a gerbil or hamster interesting. When she was twelve she'd had a tank of tropical fish for a while but although fish looked attractive at first they'd got strange fungal diseases and she'd given them away.

'Then again, you seem to have made something of a pet of that young Cultist,' Lisle said. Her voice was so reasonable that it took Laura a moment to realize what she'd said.

'Glossali?' Laura tried to put the right amount of outrage into her voice. 'He's a friend . . .'

'Spare me,' Lisle's voice snapped. 'I don't have time to fence with you, Laura Harrell. Your act doesn't convince me.'

For the first time since she'd been blinded Laura felt herself straining to see, wanting to see the expression on Lisle's face. But it was useless and she sat in silence, not knowing what sort of response was expected.

'I'm not trying to trap you,' Lisle said after a moment. 'The trial is over, you won your case and that's the end of it as far as I'm concerned. But you've set in motion events that are larger than you realize and you're woefully ill-prepared for the consequences.'

'What do you mean?' Laura asked slowly. She didn't know what kind of game Lisle was playing an[d] [s]he wasn't about to lower her guard just because [the] woman said it was safe.

'I mean that you are not the first pers[on] Collegiate law for your own purposes,' Lisl[e] 'And that you may have found it amus[ing] and defenceless but I think you'll find the reality less enjoyable.' Her voice was sharp and Laura heard a low growl of sound and felt her skin prickle with alarm.

'Are you threatening me?' she asked incredulously.

'No. Believe it or not, I'm trying to help you.' Lisle spoke quietly but with conviction. 'This part of the Library may be about to become very dangerous and your clever excuses won't help you when the weather changes.'

Laura shivered, despite herself. She wondered if maybe she'd been too hasty in casting all the blame on Alex during the trial. Her brother might not have been much of a defender but up until now she'd always been able to rely on him supporting her. Now he was gone and the other members of their group seemed to have vanished.

'You've alienated your companions,' Lisle said, echoing her thoughts. 'You've thrown your brother to the wolves and now all you have to rely upon is that naive and impressionable Catalogue Cultist. I'm offering you a way out, if you choose to take it.'

'And why should I trust you?' Laura asked sarcastically. 'You with your vague premonitions and obscure threats?' She felt herself getting angry as she added: 'I've done all right so far, haven't I?'

'Have you?' Lisle's voice seemed to hold a thread of pity. 'I heard what you said before. You may have escaped judgement but your ambitions have come to nothing. You have to start all over again.'

'And you're offering to help me?' Laura said, disbelievingly.

'I'm offering you a chance,' Lisle corrected. 'Only that. A chance to start again in another world.'

# 2

Ciren was troubled about something. Charm knew it and she felt a stab of anger when she admitted it to herself. Morgan was the problem. Morgan and Kal had always been trouble. Ever since the twins had first brought them into the Wheel something hadn't been right with Ciren. Only when they'd gone to speak to Vespertine Chalcedony, their patron, had the difficulty vanished. Then they had acted as one mind again, following Vespertine's orders to recapture Morgan and bring her to Chalice.

Now there was something wrong. Charm knew that look on her twin's face because it was one her own never wore; or had never worn until Ciren began it. She'd read his mind for the first time in her life to attempt to discover the reason for it and found herself blocked. Although she'd been able to discover that her twin secretly believed Kal and Morgan would never willingly join the Wheel, there was a grey place in Ciren's mind that she hadn't been able to touch.

She'd hoped Vespertine could remove it. When she thought back she couldn't remember exactly what Vespertine had said but he'd made her feel easy in her mind about Ciren. It was good to work as a unit again, not needing to speak to discuss what should be done, simply doing it. Killing those two Jurists had been the obvious thing to do and they'd done it. Charm felt no particular pleasure in killing, no more than fulfilling any of her patron's wishes, but she'd been pleased at how smoothly everything had worked out.

But as they travelled to Vespertine's villa, returning to Chalice for the first time in a year, she could feel the old worry rising to the surface. Ciren had acted strangely during their mission to retrieve Morgan, seeming to doubt himself even when obeying orders. So now Charm doubted as well.

Charm was watching him. Ciren felt queasy staring into those black-purple eyes that were mirrors of his own. All she needed to do was smile and she'd be inside his mind and he didn't know why he feared that as much as he did.

She'd only read his mind once. They'd never felt a need to before. Only when they had admitted something was wrong between them had she suggested it and he had agreed. He'd let her in and after that everything had changed. The old unity between them, which had once felt so natural, was back but different now. Ciren felt as if someone else was walking around in his skin. *What is this thing I am?* he asked himself, hooked on Charm's stare and unable to look away. *What is this thing I am that she is also?* He was losing himself; while sitting still in the coach somewhere inside he was falling, falling for ever. *Where am I if I'm not here?* He had to look away.

Morgan was huddled in the corner of the coach, her arms hugging her own body and her fingers digging into her skin fiercely. It made him go hot and cold to look at her: as if he, not Charm, could read her mind. How else could he know how terrified she was? She didn't want to feel and yet was desperate to feel something all at once.

What would Vespertine do with her? Could Morgan become a useful agent for the Wheel? Would she obey their patron's will as obediently as he and his twin? Every question had sent his head spinning further, sinking into a spiral that led ever further down. *How is it I feel when I don't feel like this?* He should tell Vespertine about his doubts, about this sense of having lost himself, that there was a stranger under his skin. But the thought of telling Vespertine added another lurch to the spinning and made it worse. He couldn't tell Vespertine.

Charm's eyes bored into him from across the coach and Ciren couldn't look at her. She didn't need to read his mind to know his doubts. Once she was certain she would tell Vespertine herself.

Zoë didn't like looking at the frozen figure of Kal. It was strangely like spying, she felt, seeing someone caught in a single moment. When she'd first studied his expression all she'd noticed was the anger but increasingly she thought it was more like desperation. She'd seen the boy Archon make his final plea to save Morgan and admired him for it. Now it made her feel uncomfortable to see him trapped like a fly in amber, knowing that Morgan was far away by now and there was nothing Kal could do about it.

Dalandran had left saying he would have to consult with the rest of the Jurists about what to do with Kal.

Since then Jhezra's behaviour had seemed almost callous. She had taken a notebook and pen out of a pocket of her tunic and was staring with narrowed eyes at Kal as she jotted down tiny scribbles in her book.

'What are you writing?' Zoë asked eventually and Jhezra glanced over at her briefly.

'Symptoms,' she said and Zoë blinked.

'Excuse me?'

'Perhaps that did not translate,' Jhezra said, laying down her pen and looking back at Zoë. 'But I am writing what I can see now. So that if this changes,' she gestured at the sparkling dazzle that surrounded Kal, 'then I will properly remember what went before.'

'I understand,' Zoë said slowly, silently reminding herself that Jhezra was anything but stupid. The other girl might have grown up in a nomadic society but she seemed to have grasped the culture of the Great Library better than the rest of them.

As Jhezra finished writing, Zoë looked about to see the business of the Converse Court continuing around them. A couple of speakers had mounted podiums across the hall and were haranguing their audiences, people loaded and unloaded books from the open shelves; and the occasional passer-by glanced curiously at the human statue and the two girls who watched over it.

'It looks as if they've forgotten us,' Zoë said, uncertainly.

'The Jurists do not take responsibility for their actions,' Jhezra said and her voice was heavy with disappointment. 'They judge, sometimes wisely and sometimes foolishly. But in the end they are like the other people we've met, uninterested in anything beyond their own faction.'

'Well said.' A voice spoke near by and the two girls turned to see a woman watching them. Zoë was the first to recognize her.

The woman wore a dress of embroidered patchwork sections and had a brightly coloured cloth bound through her plait of dark brown hair. She had been one of the speakers they'd listened to when they first arrived at the Court, the one who had accused the Jurists of being complacent.

'Sibalent Askew,' the woman said, nodding but not offering to shake hands. 'Peregrinade. Formerly of the Jurists.'

'I'm Zoë Kaul and this is my friend Jhezra and . . .' Zoë hesitated and then gestured at the standing statue. 'Kal.' She ran her fingers though her hair nervously, wondering how much the woman had overheard. 'We're waiting for someone to come and look at Kal but they seem to have forgotten about us.'

'As your friend is aware, they are blinkered,' the woman said. 'For a while they have been a force for order in the Library but their light is waning now.'

As she spoke Zoë's heart sank. She'd thought for a moment that Sibalent was about to offer some useful advice but now she sounded more like a doomsayer.

'My people have a saying. You can be blinded by too much light as much as too little,' Jhezra said, still watching the woman with interest.

'A philosophy that would have served the Lightbringers well,' Sibalent replied. 'They too were a faction that sought to bring order. They too failed.'

'But why?' Zoë's voice was strained and her eyes travelled back to Kal for a moment. 'When we first came here the Library seemed like the answer to all our questions but it's been worse than useless.'

'You must learn to see in the darkness,' Sibalent said, with a secretive smile.

Zoë clenched her fists, feeling herself getting angry. But Jhezra put a reassuring hand on her arm.

'What can you tell us of the Wheel faction?' she asked. 'It was their agents who took my friend Alexander away.' She glanced at Zoë before adding, 'And Morgan, who was also judged by this Court.'

'They also claim to bring order,' Sibalent said softly. 'And they hide their own darkness behind a locked Door.' She glanced swiftly around the room, checking that no one was in earshot, before stepping closer and lowering her voice. 'Your friends are in danger; for the Wheel releases no one as long as they can be useful, discarding people only when they have been used up.'

'Thank you for your warning,' Jhezra said quietly as Zoë stared.

'Seek out the Mandela,' Sibalent said, still speaking softly. 'The darkness and dust of the Library vanishes when you come out into the light of day.' Then she stepped back from them and within moments she was lost in the crowd.

Zoë turned to Jhezra, a question on her lips. But the other girl shook her head quickly, looking up from the notebook she'd been scrawling in, and raised a hand to press a finger to her lips. Moving closer she bent her head to Zoë's ear and said quietly, 'We're in danger as well,' she said. 'As long as we don't understand what's happening here.' Moving away she added, 'We must find someone to help us. Someone we can trust.'

Alex waited for ten minutes in the plain room but it felt like a hundred years. The brave thing to do would be to leave, the daring thing to do would be to escape, but Alex did the cowardly thing and stayed. He told himself he was being sensible. Discretion is the better part of valour, and all that jazz. But really he was scared.

When the door opened again he wasn't really

surprised when the new arrival turned out to be the commander who had been at the Door. He was a burly man with grizzled grey hair and a short beard and he looked Alex up and down before speaking.

'Name.'

'Alexander Harrell, sir.' He felt himself relax a bit despite the peremptory question. Army discipline was something he could understand.

'Collegiate member?'

'No, sir.' The commander frowned instead of going on to the next question and Alex had time to continue. 'They haven't done me any favours, sir.'

'Do you know where you are, boy?' the commander asked, more slowly, and Alex realized the man had departed from the catechism he'd prepared.

'Not really, sir.'

'What's that supposed to mean?' The commander's eyes were narrowed with suspicion and Alex knew he wouldn't get a better time to explain himself.

'I was told this world was called Chalice. That it belonged to someone called Chalcedony and to the faction of the Wheel. But I don't know what that means, sir.'

The commander was silent for a moment and Alex tried to breathe calmly. It was difficult when he knew so little of what this man wanted. Had it been foolish to disclaim a relationship with the Collegiate or would the gamble pay off? He knew the Wheel broke Collegiate rules so it had seemed sensible to put himself on their side. But perhaps he'd lost his only chance to claim the protection of those rules.

The commander hrumphed thoughtfully and then trained his steely glare back on Alex.

'What worlds have you been on?'

'I was born on Earth, sir. Then a world controlled by

a government called the Tetrarchate, a peasant village on another world, then the Collegiate Library, then here. Sir.'

'Factions you visited in the Library?' the commander demanded and Alex guessed they'd returned to the catechism.

'Uh, the Catalogue Cult were the first I met, then the Jurists. But I met some other people who seemed to belong to more than one.' He thought back, trying to remember. 'Scholars and . . . um . . . Pilgrims, I think . . .'

'Any skills?' The commander cut him off and Alex flushed, realizing that he'd been rambling.

'I know how to use a sword. Sir.' His right hand clenched slightly and the commander surprised him with a sudden boom of laughter.

'We'll give you a sword,' he said. 'You're scheduled for Salvage, lad. Know what that means?'

'No, sir.' Alex shook his head.

'Means, whatever you've done, someone in the Wheel thinks you're worth salvaging. It's up to you to prove whether they were right.'

'Yes, sir.' Alex felt himself heave a sigh of relief and knew the commander had seen it. It didn't matter. Salvage wasn't a sentence, it was a reprieve.

The commander nodded and then took a step back, looking at Alex assessingly.

'Right then. Your dormitory is beta-one in the east quarter of the barracks. The quartermaster will get you kitted out and you'll train with the rest of your squad until the arms-master gets an idea of your level. You'll attend initiation classes until the council of the Wheel decides to induct you.'

'Yes, sir.'

'You'll obey orders, keep your hands clean, and don't get a smart mouth. Understood?'

'Yessir.' Alex tried the salute he'd seen earlier and the commander saluted back.

'Dismissed,' he said and under his watchful eyes, Alex walked to the door of the plain room and hauled it open.

Outside, the dim grey light and the crunch of the gravel path beneath his feet felt like paradise. I'm alive, he thought to himself. It was hard to care about what might happen next in comparison with what he'd just been through. Right then he was grateful enough to do anything the Wheel wanted him to.

Laura leant lightly against the wall of the Court. Around her she could hear the sound of people coming and going and speakers lecturing from points around the wide expanse of the room. When the Court had pronounced her innocent Dalandran had advised her to seek out an experienced world-traveller to help her learn about the Collegiate. Now it seemed that Lisle was offering to be that person.

'You make it sound very appealing,' she said. 'But I'm not interested in starting again. I'd rather build on what I already know. For example, the fact that every Collegiate member has their own agenda.' She lifted her head to face towards where she thought Lisle's face was and added: 'What's your agenda, Lisle Weft? Why should you offer to help me?'

Lisle laughed quietly, and Laura stiffened at the thought that she was being mocked.

'Why should you believe me, whatever I tell you?' Lisle asked. 'But for what it's worth, I came into the Library for the first time when I was your age. I also longed for power and for revenge.'

Laura waited but Lisle had stopped speaking and she said cautiously, 'Go on . . .'

'What more is there to say?' Lisle asked. 'I'm here. I know the Library, I know the Collegiate, I'm trusted by the Jurists and by those from other stranger factions. And if you come with me you'll see what status I hold on my own world as well.'

'I'll see?' Laura asked with an edge of sarcasm and Lisle replied at once.

'Yes. You'll see.' Her voice was confident with certainty that this was one offer Laura would not refuse. 'My world has very little magic. Only enough to work the simplest translation spell or witch-light. The curse that blinds your eyes will have no power there.'

Laura tried not to react, guessing how closely the woman was watching her. She already knew what she was going to answer. What choice did she have? The only Collegiate members she knew here were Lisle and Glossali and she wasn't about to join the Catalogue Cult. Asking a stranger for help wasn't much of a prospect, either; at least with Lisle she knew a little about how the woman operated.

'And if I agree?' she said. 'What will you want in return?'

'Your co-operation,' Lisle said seriously. 'And courtesy towards your former travelling companions. For I shall endeavour to persuade them to join me as well.'

'Jhezra and Zoë?' Laura was incredulous. 'After what happened in the trial they'd never agree to travel with me.' She frowned. 'And why do you want *them*? They're useless. What game are you playing, Lisle?'

'No game.' Lisle's voice held a snap of anger. 'What happens here is real and dangerous. You and your companions have stumbled into a darkness you don't yet understand.'

This time it was Laura who laughed.

'With respect,' she said, 'I think I've had enough of

cryptic words from the Collegiate. What danger are you talking about? What is it that you think I should fear?'

She had thought Lisle might take offence but if anything her tone was approving when she replied.

'Others who twist the laws of the Collegiate with greater facility than you, Laura Harrell,' she said. 'They call themselves The Wheel.'

The coach rolled to a halt and stopped with a final jerk. Morgan hadn't looked out of the window and when Charm opened the coach door, the light hurt her eyes. Her head ached and her face felt tight and swollen and she stumbled as Ciren helped her down the steps.

The coach had stopped on the roadway where a wide gravel path lay off at right angles to a building on the right. Morgan's eyes swam as she tried to focus on it and it wasn't until they were walking towards it that she realized the gravel path crossed a flat expanse of water on its way to the double doors of the entrance. There were fish in the water; Morgan could see their silvery shapes beneath the surface and, remembering a fountain in a garden on a distant world, she felt the tears starting again.

The double doors stood open and the twins walked inside, escorting her between them. Inside was cool and shadowy and two figures appeared out of the dimness and bowed. They wore loose fitting clothes in grey and their feet were bare, walking silently across the stone floor.

'Master Ciren, Mistress Charm. The Lord Vespertine bade me wish you welcome home.' The servant's words pattered lightly on the air.

'This is Morgan who will be a guest here,' Ciren was

saying and Morgan felt his hand on her arm as he spoke again. 'Morgan? Would you like to rest, to sleep? Or something to eat perhaps?'

She looked at him, wondering why he thought it mattered what she wanted, and Charm shifted suddenly to give her a little push towards the servants.

The grey servant and his companion took her arms and Morgan had an impulse to pull away and run. But there was nowhere to run to. She let them lead her across the hall and away down another cool dim passageway and into another room.

'Here is a bed, lady,' one of the servants said. 'Shall I remove your shoes?' He didn't wait for an answer, kneeling on the floor and starting to unlace Morgan's boots.

'I will fetch refreshment,' said the other one, moving away. He didn't seem to expect a reply and Morgan felt strangely soothed by it. These people didn't need her to answer them. They only spoke to tell her what they were doing.

'I will put your shoes in this cupboard, lady,' the remaining servant said, although Morgan didn't turn her head. 'Here is also a sleeping robe for you. If you will excuse me for one moment I will draw a bath in the next room.'

Morgan waited, sitting on the edge of the bed, while the servant crossed to the other side of the room and opened a door, leaving it ajar when he passed through. On the other side Morgan heard a splash and then a gush of falling water. The room was dark grey stone but the bed and the cupboard and the other pieces of furniture were white. The 'sleeping robe' the servant had laid out beside her on the bed was a watery grey silk, like the silver-scaled bodies of the fish.

She was looking up when the servant returned

through the open door and thought perhaps it wasn't a man. The servant's face was squarish and the skin smooth and clean. She or he was no taller than Morgan or the twins, less than full adult height, but somehow didn't seem like a child either. As the other door opened Morgan looked to see the second servant enter carrying a tray. This one looked like the first, not with the eerie duplication of the twins, but different features that also could have been masculine or feminine.

'Here is water and fruit for you, lady,' the servant with the tray said, putting it down on a table, covered with a white cloth. He poured water from a flagon into a glass and brought it carefully across the room, fitting her hand to it when he reached her. 'Will you drink a little?'

She wasn't sure which of them really lifted the glass but when it knocked against her lips and teeth she opened her mouth and managed to swallow. It was cold and burned her throat going down.

'Will you take some fruit?' the servant asked and Morgan managed to shake her head slightly, releasing the half empty glass back into his hands.

'You're cold. Let me help you with your robe.' The servant who had taken off her boots for her put the silk robe around her shoulders over her other clothes and together they guided her arms through slits in the side.

'The bath is this way,' one of them said and they lifted her to her feet, walking her slowly across the room and through the door to another plain room. The bath was a white pool raised up from the floor and they sat her down on the edge while they explained the bathroom to her.

'This is where you may relieve yourself, this basin holds water for cleansing the hands or face, and here are linens for drying the parts of the body.'

'Will you be private now, lady?' Morgan didn't say anything and the servants paused for only a moment.

'I will be at the door if you require me,' one of them said.

'I will make your bed ready,' added the other.

They left her sitting on the side of the bath and Morgan turned to look at it hopelessly. Eventually she pulled off the robe and her clothes, dropping them on the floor anywhere, and walked into the bath. The water was clear and lukewarm, deep enough to reach her waist when she stood in it. The bath was stone and a shelf inside ran round it at knee height and she sat down and then lay back, letting herself float. Her hair swirled out around her head and the water soothed her headache as her thoughts drifted.

With her head half under water she couldn't hear and when she closed her eyes she couldn't see either. It was easy to imagine falling asleep. The water got colder but underneath it was almost warm.

'Lady?'

She opened her eyes to see one of the servants standing at the edge of the bath holding a folded towel.

'Will you come out now, lady?'

Her head surfaced properly as she put her feet on the floor of the bath and the servant wrapped the towel around her in a quick impersonal motion. The discarded clothes on the floor had been removed but the other servant was holding the silk robe, not crumpled at all, unless it was another identical one. Together they helped her into it and tied it with a sash around her waist.

When they brought her back into the other room the lights had been dimmed further and the tray of fruit brought closer to the bed, the sheets drawn back invitingly.

'Will you sleep now, lady?' someone asked as Morgan approached the bed.

She hadn't thought it was possible but after her bath she was exhausted and the sheets looked cool and clean. Her eyes closed as soon as her head hit the pillow.

Vespertine Chalcedony's study was a room without windows. It was at the very centre of his villa and, although there were four doors, each leading to a different quarter of his residence, no natural light could penetrate to the heart of his home.

The long corridor the twins followed to reach the study reminded them of the Great Library, but instead of being shelved with books, thick hangings curtained the walls, swathing them in abstract patterns of light and dark. The entrance to the study was hidden behind one of the curtains and Charm reached out and drew it aside, revealing a plain wooden door. Ciren knocked, and a voice said, 'Enter.'

Inside, the room was dimly lit. Vespertine's eyesight was all but gone, his eyes screened by a milky whiteness, and he had little use for reading. The books he owned were arrayed throughout the Library section of the Wheel and, if he possessed secret tomes of knowledge, they were not displayed here. Instead the study was curtained from wall to wall, the floor carpeted and the ceiling lined with the same fabric.

There was only one chair. On rare occasions Vespertine might require his servants to place another in this room, so that a trusted Wheel member might also sit down. But whenever the twins had come to this room they had found Vespertine Chalcedony sitting alone, as he was now, sunk deep in thought and staring into blank space.

'My children,' he said, his head lifting to look at them as the twins entered. 'You have accomplished your mission then?'

'Forgive us, Vespertine,' Ciren began and the lines of his patron's face drew together like a crumpled piece of paper.

'Our mission was accomplished in part only,' Charm explained. 'Morgan is even now being attended to by your servants but Kal put himself beyond our reach.'

Vespertine's expression smoothed and the line of his thin lips expressed satisfaction.

'And the item he wears?' he asked and Charm shook her head.

'We could not retrieve it,' she confessed.

'Well, no matter,' Vespertine told them. 'The girl was most crucial. You have done well, my children.' Laying his ancient hands on the arms of his chair he nodded to the twins. 'Come here and sit with me.'

The twins came forward to kneel on either side of his chair and the founder of the Wheel looked down at them with an appearance of satisfaction.

'It has been a long time since you last came home to me,' he said softly, his voice rustling like reeds in the wind. 'Now that you are here I will keep you close by.'

# 3

Jhezra wondered what time it was, not that time meant much in the warren-like corridors of the Great Library. Since leaving her own world she'd lost track of the separation between day and night. In the desert she'd always been aware of the time: during the day as the burning sun marched up and down the sky and during the night as the frozen stars stared down from the roof of the world. The Library was a dim twilit world of lamplight and witch-globes where walls and books receded into shadowy distances and it became difficult to remember when you'd last eaten or slept.

Sibalent Askew had departed some time ago and there had been no sign of Dalandran returning. Jhezra was wondering whether to dare the *static electricity* Zoë had mentioned and try to take Kal away from this place herself. But his frozen figure would be difficult to carry even regardless of the weight he would be. She was just about to suggest that they attempt it when a change in the light caught her attention and she saw a familiar figure approaching. Lisle Weft was coming towards them, accompanied by one of the other Jurists, two of the glowing light spheres trailing after them high in the air.

'Zoë, look,' she said quickly, and they turned to look at the newcomers.

'Jhezra, Zoë,' Lisle said, nodding to them. The reddish dog she normally travelled with was no longer with her and Jhezra wondered briefly what had happened to it. 'Dalandran informed me of what has befallen the young Archon.' She looked at Kal thoughtfully before turning to indicate her companion. 'This is Tan Ecesis, a friend of mine. He is a magician.'

'You've come to help Kal?' Zoë asked, her voice rushed with relief. 'Dalandran said he didn't know how to remove the spell.'

'Unfortunately, no more do I,' the magician said with an air of apology. 'But Lisle had an idea that may help. She knows a world where magic effects are greatly lessened. If we can convey this young man there the spell may release him.'

'That sounds like a wise plan,' Jhezra said cautiously. 'But if you'll forgive me we have found the help of the Jurists somewhat double-edged thus far and I feel a certain responsibility towards Kal since we were tried and judged together. What is this world you speak of and how far away does it lie?'

'Not far,' Lisle said. 'A few hours' walk through the Library. But if you are concerned for Kal's wellbeing you would be welcome to accompany me there. In fact I rather hoped to persuade you to join us.'

'Thank you.' Zoë sounded grateful, responding to the kindness in Lisle's voice, but Jhezra had been on her guard ever since the Peregrinade had given them a warning.

'I also thank you,' she said. 'But we will need to know more before we can agree to come with you.'

Lisle paused for a moment, her expression thoughtful, and Tan Ecesis waited patiently beside her.

'When we first met you were honest with me, Jhezra,' Lisle said. 'And Zoë, you spoke in good faith to the Court. I think, though, that you have now learnt a sad lesson that honesty is not always rewarded. Just as Laura Harrell has learnt that there is more than one way of telling the truth.'

'Laura lied,' Zoë said hotly and Lisle sighed.

'Not according to the magic of the Court,' she said. 'But I admit to you that I was disappointed by the verdict. I argued against it and would have done more had I known what the result would be.' She looked again at Kal before adding, 'But all Collegiate justice is inevitably imperfect. The Great Library is ancient, its inhabitants old, its knowledge decaying. Its rules are tattered fragments of a lost system of laws.'

'Then why do you bother?' Zoë asked, still angry. 'Why are you a member of the Jurists if you don't believe in any of all this?'

'Because each of us tries to hold back chaos for as long as we can,' Lisle said simply. 'I think something we all have in common is the wish to protect what's ours . . . to keep a small space that's safe amid the turmoil of the universe.'

'What are you trying to say?' Jhezra asked, frowning.

'That this place is no longer safe,' Lisle replied.

There were always options. Alex tried to remember that. There was always something you could do, even when it seemed that events had blocked you into a corner. But already he could tell that Chalice was not a place to allow much choice about what happened to you.

He'd followed the officer's directions between the forbiddingly grey buildings along another neat gravel path and found himself in a dormitory. There were twenty beds, ten on each long side of the room. At the foot of each was a locked wooden trunk. All but three of the beds had been made with a text-book neatness which Alex regarded uneasily. The remaining ones had a pile of folded blankets on the thin pallet-type mattress and the wooden trunks at the bed foot had their keys still in the lock.

Alex selected one next to an occupied bed and opened the trunk. He'd been expecting it to be empty and it was, but on the underside of the lid a piece of paper had been pasted. *'Inventory,'* it read. *'As supplied by Quartermaster.'* Beneath was a list of items in precise script. *'Two shirts, two pairs of trousers, one standard tunic, one pair of boots, one belt, one cloak, one tinder-light, one standard knife, one standard sabre, one book.'*

Alex looked at this for a while. Then he moved to the bed and started making it up, trying to mimic the neat arrangement of the one next to him. He wasn't enjoying the sense of being conscripted but it was clear he wasn't going to achieve anything by refusing what he was obviously expected to do. He was just tucking in the final corner of the blankets when there was a rumble of noise from the hallway and a group of people came suddenly into the room.

They were men. All young, he noted with a feeling of relief. None of them looked more than five or six years older than him. They were wearing the same grey uniform of the soldiers he'd already seen but without the black and red insignia of the Wheel. They noticed him immediately but all except one of them only glanced at him as they crossed to their individual beds. The final arrival stopped in front of Alex and looked at him.

'New recruit?' he asked.

'I was ordered to report here,' Alex said. The stranger was dark-skinned with thick black hair, chopped off straight at his shoulders. He was shorter than Alex but bigger built and his confident stance was intimidating.

'That's obvious,' the stranger said. 'Or you wouldn't be here.' Alex tried to remember how he'd dealt with the young warriors of the Hajhim and steeled his shoulders.

'I'm scheduled for Salvage,' he said. 'Whatever that is.'

'It's a loyalty test.' The boy's mouth twisted in a smirking way. 'Unless you pass it you're not in the Wheel, you just belong to it.'

'Are you in the Wheel?' Alex asked and the boy's smirk shifted into a sneer.

'*We're* in Orientation Training,' he said, emphasizing the words. 'You only get Salvaged if you're from a Rogue faction or a Renegade group.' He took a step forward into Alex's space and spoke louder as he added: 'I'm Reck, the leader of this squad.'

'Alex Iskander Harrell,' Alex said, reviving his old Hajhi nickname on a sudden whim. Reck might be bigger than him but that didn't necessarily mean he'd seen any more combat.

'Alexiskander,' Reck repeated, his eyes narrowing. 'Sounds like a sneeze.'

A couple of the other recruits laughed and Alex briefly considered objecting or pointing out that Reck's name sounded like gagging. But he didn't risk it and stayed silent instead.

'Well?' Reck said and Alex stood his ground.

'Well what?'

Reck sneered again but the other recruits had finished changing clothes and were buckling on swords as they headed for the door and Reck himself cursed under his breath, turning away from Alex.

'Hurry up and get your gear, then find us in the armoury,' he ordered, heading after the others. 'You're not one of this squad until we see how you handle a sword.'

It was strange to be back in Lisle Weft's study. Only that morning Jhezra had read the sign at the entrance: 'Lisle Weft of Fenrisnacht, Jurist'. Lisle had helped them at first and then, in the Converse Court, been part of the group that judged them. Now she was offering them a safe haven but Jhezra still wasn't sure how much she could be trusted.

The room smelt of foreign spices; a pleasant smell compared to the dusty stale air of most of the Library. Sitting in a high-backed armchair, Laura was sipping a fresh cup of tea and Zoë was as far away from her as she could manage, eyeing her angrily from across the room. Lisle had persuaded them to rest here while she arranged for Kal's unconscious body to be transported to the nearby study of the magician Tan Ecesis. However, when they'd arrived they'd found Laura waiting with the dog, Pepper, sitting next to her.

'What are you doing here?' Zoë had demanded and Laura had lifted her head to look in their direction. She was getting better at pretending sight although her clear green eyes were as unreadable as ever.

'Lisle invited me to travel with her,' she said. 'And to anticipate your next question, I don't know why. Perhaps you should ask her to explain when she gets back?'

'You bet I will,' Zoë had muttered, throwing herself down in another chair and glaring mutinously at Laura. The dog had pricked up its ears at the suppressed anger in her voice but made no other movement.

Jhezra wondered if Pepper had been set to guard Laura or perhaps Lisle's possessions. In the desert some tribes kept animals for defence, but not of this type. Still, although this creature seemed perfectly tamed to Lisle's command the set of its ears and the alert look in its eye led Jhezra to suspect it might be on watch.

'How can you just sit there?' Zoë blurted out, interrupting Jhezra's musings and swinging round to stare at Laura, plainly about to launch into another tirade against her former friend.

'Very easily,' Laura said with a calm tone that Jhezra knew was calculated to infuriate Zoë.

Zoë gasped and suddenly Jhezra didn't have the patience to listen to this all over again. After having made excuses for Laura ever since the fall of Shattershard Zoë now seemed unable to spend any time in her company without it degenerating into a fight.

'Zoë, may I speak with you privately?' she asked and was rewarded with a look of surprise from Zoë and Laura's head twitching in her direction.

'Um, yes, OK,' Zoë said and Jhezra stood up. There was another room leading off this one, screened by a curtain. But, with a glance at Laura and the dog, she decided against that option.

'Let us step out into the corridor,' she said. 'Excuse us, Laura.'

'Oh, don't mind me,' Laura said lightly.

'We won't,' Zoë snapped but she followed Jhezra out of the study. The dog watched them but didn't move and Jhezra felt slightly relieved. If it had prevented them from leaving she would not have dared do more than defend herself. There was almost certain to be a Library law that she'd be breaking if she damaged someone's dog.

Out in the corridor she led Zoë several metres down between the book-lined shelves. She didn't want Laura to overhear what she was about to say.

'What is it?' Zoë asked and Jhezra took a slow breath.

'This argument between you and Laura serves no purpose,' she said. Zoë's light-brown eyes went round with shock and Jhezra gritted her teeth and continued. 'Please hear me out, my friend. Believe me, I say this only to help you.'

'OK.' Zoë wetted her lips and smiled uneasily. 'Go on. I'll listen.'

'Thank you.' Jhezra met Zoë's eyes, hoping that the other girl would be able to understand her point. Zoë was her friend but they came from such different cultures.

Jhezra was used to giving and taking orders without argument. Explaining her thought processes was something she'd only really done with Alex when teaching him about her world. Now she needed to teach Zoë something about a situation that was strange to them both.

'Zoë, you must stop thinking of Laura as a person from your world,' she began. 'This is what the Jurists said that Kal and I must do. That we must not think of each other as the Archon of Shattershard and a warrior of the tribes. If the Jurists had given you good advice I believe they would have told you this as well. Laura is not a girl from this school that you remember. She is something else entirely.'

'But that's what I've been saying . . .' Zoë began and Jhezra raised a hand to halt her.

'No. Forgive me, but it is not.' She watched Zoë

swallow and continued quickly. 'The desert I came from and this Great Library are very different places from your world. In both of these places Laura has achieved much. Yes, she has also destroyed much.' She nodded to the objection she knew Zoë would make. 'If I had known then what I know now, I would never have agreed to be a part of her plans. But you must admit that she has used her talents to great effect.'

'But that's what's so awful about it,' Zoë said and Jhezra could hear the unshed tears in her voice.

'I know, my friend. And if you simply cannot bear to spend time in her company I will understand. But I need you to listen to all I have to say first.'

'Yes, I'm sorry, go on.' Zoë blinked and then drew herself together, concentrating.

Jhezra felt a rush of affection for her, simply because she was prepared to listen to something she didn't want to hear.

'Zoë, you must accept this new reality. Laura is not your friend to be chided at what you see as her bad behaviour. Imagine her as a stranger, one who could be an ally or an enemy.'

Zoë's face got a thoughtful look and Jhezra pressed on.

'She is someone who wants power and privilege. She has no interest in returning to her own world, instead she wants to find one where her intelligence will allow her to dominate others.'

'That's something that's against the Collegiate rules, isn't it?' Zoë said and Jhezra nodded.

'So they would have us believe,' she said, flashing her friend a quick smile. 'But we know the rules are not the same for every faction and I am certain Laura is currently contriving ways to hide her plans from the Collegiate.'

'I just bet she is,' Zoë agreed with an edge of bitterness and Jhezra hastened to continue.

'But this is Laura's talent,' she said. 'And see how she has used it . . .' She spoke with conviction as she tried to show Zoë what had become clear to her. 'On my own world Laura's plans changed everything for both myself and for Kal. Here in the Library while you and I and Alex stumbled about in confusion, Laura understood everything and made another plan without us even knowing it.'

'We were stupid,' Zoë said and Jhezra shrugged.

'We did not see what was right in front of us,' she said. 'Or perhaps being blind allowed Laura to guess what was hidden. It doesn't matter.'

'Doesn't matter?' Zoë looked surprised.

'The past is past. Now, we must look at the future. What are our plans? What do we wish to achieve? Who are our allies and who are our enemies?'

'So you're saying that I need to decide about Laura.'

'Yes, among other things,' Jhezra agreed. 'Decide as if she were a stranger. Shall we make a pact with her or shall we oppose her?'

When Vespertine dismissed them Ciren and Charm went to their suite of rooms in the southern side of the villa. Whenever they were not travelling the worlds or working for their faction in the Great Library, this was where they lived.

Ciren had never thought of this as home. As far as he knew he had no home world, although Vespertine had adopted him and Charm as his own. He'd seen the palaces and mansions that other senior members of the Wheel possessed and they'd all contained something of their owner's to identify them: trophies, or treasure, or some other item they personally valued. This suite, like all of his patron's residence, was impersonal. Anyone might use these rooms although, as far as Ciren knew, no one but he and his twin ever did.

Charm seemed comfortable enough, ordering food and wine from the servants and soaking away the dust of the journey in the bathroom. Ciren had eaten and washed and dressed himself in fresh clothing but now he found it difficult to settle down to sleep. In their room in the Library he kept the books that interested him and the paper notes he made when working out his own thoughts about them. Now he did not even have the journal he and his twin kept of their travels. They had turned that over to Vespertine, as they always did.

'What troubles you?' Charm asked, coming into the room as he sat on the side of his bed.

'There is nothing of mine here,' he said, answering the question instinctively before looking up to see the frown on her face.

'A strange thing to say,' she said. Like him, she wore a plain black sleep robe and she held a glass of wine almost as dark, which she sipped from as she considered him. 'We did not bring much with us this time, it is true. But you know you can request anything you want from the servants.'

'I know.' Ciren shook his head. 'It was a foolish thought.'

'But you felt it,' Charm replied. 'So it must be real to you.'

Ciren looked at her, wondering if she would suggest that he take his troubles to Vespertine. Instead she handed him her glass of wine and said, 'Wait here a moment.'

She turned and went back into the outer room and

within a moment was back again, carrying his bow in one hand and his black cloak folded over her arm.

'See,' she said, glancing at him as she hung the cloak on a hookstand across the room and then carefully placed his bow on the bare surface of the empty desk. 'That is your cloak and your weapon. Now there are two things here that belong to you. Do you want me to fetch your gauntlets also?'

'No, that won't be necessary.' Ciren couldn't help smiling and an answering light in Charm's eyes brought back the memory of happier days.

'And that is *my* glass of wine.' Charm turned and collected it from his hand, nodding at him as she drank again from the glass. 'If you want your own there is more in the pitcher next door.'

Ciren followed her suggestion more by reflex than because he wanted wine. But he poured a small amount into a second glass and drank, the thick liquid coating his tongue with dark spices. When he came back Charm was sitting on her own bed and she favoured him with a thoughtful look.

'Tomorrow, if Vespertine does not require our services, perhaps you would like to ride?' she suggested. 'The servants say the weather is expected to be fine.'

'Yes.' Ciren imagined himself riding, testing his horse against Charm's as they raced over the surface of the world. 'That sounds pleasant,' he agreed.

'Good then.' Charm nodded and took a last sip from her glass before putting it aside. 'Vespertine is pleased with our success. I shouldn't imagine he would object.'

'Yes,' Ciren agreed.

But as Charm composed herself for sleep he felt uneasy once more. He took another sip of the wine and almost gagged at the taste, metallic and cloying in his mouth. He turned to look once more at his bow and thought instead of Charm's flashing blades cutting down the Jurists. His cloak was a patch of black in the dim room and the red and black symbol of the Wheel winked at him from the heavy folds.

Vespertine was pleased. He knew he should be content with that. But instead his self-doubt seemed more pronounced than ever.

Laura heard the clatter of the bead curtain that hung across the entrance to Lisle's study and tilted her head up. Only one set of footsteps walked in with a long confident stride.

'Jhezra,' she said.

'I'm not surprised you recognize my walk,' the Hajhi girl said and Laura heard her come closer and the creak of a chair and a scuff of boots against the floor. 'I have heard that those who lose their sight can gain better hearing because of all they must listen for.'

'Where's Zoë?' Laura said, cutting through this and there was a pause.

'Waiting outside. She has asked me to speak to you for her.'

'Why?'

Laura was suspicious. She knew of course that Zoë had annexed the Hajhi girl but she wasn't used to Jhezra intervening in her own relationship with Zoë. It was hard to forget that Jhezra was the dangerous one. She carried that scimitar constantly and knew how to use it.

'Is this going to be more about what a terrible person I am?' Laura asked and Jhezra paused before replying.

'No, this is something new. Zoë and I have discussed this and she wants you to know that she is willing to travel with you only if you will share your plans with us.'

'What?' Laura felt caught off-guard. 'What plans?' she asked, wondering what Jhezra thought she was intending. Wasn't what she'd achieved so far enough?

'We can guess at some of them already,' Jhezra told her. 'We know you don't plan to return to Earth. I would imagine you still hope to cure your blindness but perhaps you really don't consider that an injury.'

'Not an injury?' Laura felt a flood of anger, not so much at what Jhezra was saying but at the fact that she couldn't think of any adequate response. It was all so different from the other girl's usual behaviour.

'We would like you to share your plans,' Jhezra repeated. 'And to suspend hostilities with Zoë. She is willing to do the same.'

'And why should I care?' Laura asked, finally finding her voice. 'Why should I care what Zoë thinks or about what either of you do?'

'Because you know that you can trust us,' Jhezra said but there was a dangerous note in her voice as she added, 'You've taken advantage of that in the past. You know that if we travel with you we will guide you honestly. Is there anyone else who you trust to do that?'

Laura thought about it. Until now she'd only considered Zoë and Jhezra an unfortunate complication in her plans. After the trial she was sure Zoë at least hated her for escaping any blame. But now they were offering to help her and she had to admit that with Zoë as her eyes and Jhezra's scimitar defending her, she'd feel safer than travelling alone with Lisle.

'Why is Zoë suggesting this?' she asked slowly. 'She hates me.'

'She has a problem with your attitude,' Jhezra said, the words sounding odd within the rest of her speech, translated through the magical amulets they both wore.

'But she accepts that you are better able to understand the customs of other worlds.'

'So she's going to make up and be friends?' Laura couldn't help smiling.

'No. But if you deal fairly with us we will accept you as an ally.'

Morgan lay in the darkness. She had slept and dreamed of being encased in cold grey stone and woken without knowing it. The silence of the room rang in her ears and the silken sheets were cool and slippery like water. She had struggled while she slept and her arms and legs were trapped in folds of cloth pinning her to the bed.

The vision of her dream lay on her still and she struggled again to free herself and half fell out of the bed as she escaped. The thin white carpet beneath her did not block out the cold of the stone floor below and she shivered convulsively.

Her hands clenched, nails digging into her palms, and as she stood up she could feel the panic fluttering inside her. Kal was gone, worlds away. She imagined the distance like the black void of space, an immensity that nearly crushed her to the floor again with its vastness. Instead she walked forward and saw her own reflection come swimming towards her from across the room out of the silvered glass of a mirror.

The long grey robe concealed her from her neck to her ankles, her feet white and cold beneath the silk as she crossed the room to look at herself. Her hair was loose and fell in lank hanks of oily black over her shoulders and down her back. Her eyes were shadowed and the skin underneath looked bruised and Morgan felt a pang as she met her own gaze.

She'd thought the further away from home she was,

the happier she'd be. Now she was a million miles away from home and she had a hopeless longing for her own world. In her room with the damp stain on the wall and the cramped bookcase with her collection of books she could have hidden under the duvet and cried, as she had so many times before, trying to wish her troubles away. She'd wished for magic, and the power to show everyone the consequences of being cruel to her. Well, she'd got her wish.

Kal was gone. In her dream he'd been dead. Wherever he was, she couldn't imagine him coming to find her. All her life no one had ever cared as much as he had. With him, she'd felt safe and protected. Still staring at herself in the mirror Morgan knew that without him, she was nothing. Whatever power she'd had within her when she stood with Kal at the wall of Shattershard, she didn't have it now.

Zoë had been looking without interest at the books which lined the corridor outside Lisle's study. Her mind was still trying to come to terms with what she and Jhezra had agreed to do about Laura and wondering why Lisle was offering to help them. A sound further down the passageway made her turn and she blinked when she saw what was coming towards her.

Something that looked like a crystal coffin was sliding down the corridor at about waist-height, despite the fact that there was nothing supporting it. As Zoë stared at the object she could just make out a shape through the icy-grey surface and realized that it must be Kal's body. Behind the coffin was Lisle Weft, obviously able to keep the thing moving forward while only touching it lightly.

Zoë came closer, trying to make out Kal's face inside the crystal, and Lisle nodded to her.

'Tan Ecesis was able to create this,' she said. 'Using his own magic to surround Kal. What do you think?'

'Like Snow White,' Zoë said and then blushed. 'Then your friend couldn't break the spell?'

'No, but he had an idea as to who might be able to. At least in this form, the boy is movable. At my age I'm not about to carry him over my shoulder.'

'So you still plan to take him with you?' Zoë said slowly. 'To this world you say is safe. And us. And Laura.'

'Yes.' Lisle looked at her levelly. 'As far as the Jurists are concerned Kal could stay a statue in the Converse Court for ever. Since he cannot help himself, I will do the best by him that I can.' She paused. 'And the best by you. That is, if you've made up your mind to come with me.'

'I'm thinking about it,' Zoë said, meeting the older woman's eyes. 'But you haven't told us where you're going yet.'

'Back to my own world,' Lisle said, her expression unreadable. 'To Fenrisnacht.'

# 4

Zoë and her companions left the Library the next day. Lisle had not taken long to get ready, leaving the furnishings of her study behind. Zoë had wondered out loud if they would be safe but the elderly woman had shrugged.

'I'll worry about that when I come back,' she said and Zoë caught the implication that she doubted if she would return at all.

They had slept for a few hours on palettes on the floor of an empty room near by. As always it was impossible to tell the difference between night and day in the Library but Zoë had needed the rest and had slept like a log until Jhezra gently shook her awake with the news that Lisle was ready to leave. Laura was already awake and re-tying a scarf across her eyes. As Zoë changed into her spare shirt and bundled her few possessions into her kitbag, she watched Laura carefully remaking the palette bed by feel alone.

Laura hadn't yet agreed to be honest with them but

after talking to Jhezra yesterday, Zoë was now clearer in her own mind about their relationship. Privately she could admit that Laura was better at being a Collegiate member than she was herself. *But it's because she's selfish,* she told herself. *She doesn't really obey the rules, she just pretends to.* Zoë wondered if she could pretend to believe in something like that and doubted it.

It was the kind of thing she used to discuss with her father and, as she finished collecting her things, she stroked the sleeve of the cream coat he had brought her back from Germany. Soldiers didn't argue with orders no matter what they might privately think; but her father had once said he didn't think a person had any business joining the army if they disagreed with its essential principles.

*'There's no place for a conscientious objector in a military force,'* he used to say. *'Or anyone who needs to stop and think if the cause is just before picking up a gun. There's nothing wrong with making up your own mind about things but when other people are relying on you isn't the time for that. On the battlefield, uncertainty will get you killed.'*

That was really the reason why Laura had triumphed over the rest of them, Zoë realized. While she and Jhezra and even Alex had foundered over endless alternatives, Laura's plans never had any room for doubts.

When they joined Lisle outside her study, Zoë wondered if she was making the same mistake again in agreeing to travel with the Jurist woman. She'd done her best to think the decision through but in the end she'd had to accept she still didn't know enough. Although she hoped Lisle was trustworthy she had no way to know for sure. All she could do was try to prepare for what might happen in the future so that neither Laura nor anyone else would be able to catch her off-guard.

It seemed that Lisle was also not taking any chances. As their small group assembled in the corridor, they kept their voices down. Around them, the bustle of the Jurist section was hushed.

'The other Jurists with studies on this corridor meet together for breakfast at about this time,' she explained quietly. 'If we leave now, they won't ask any awkward questions.'

'Do they know you're leaving?' Laura asked and Lisle glanced only briefly in her direction.

'Some do,' she said. 'But not many would care. I often come and go without notice.' Her voice was deliberately casual but Zoë guessed that, this time, Lisle was relieved to attract so little attention.

The crystal coffin that held Kal's body had been left in Lisle's rooms during the night. Now it, too, had been prepared for travel and was covered with a heavy blanket made of white-tipped fur.

'The second spell, which Tan Ecesis cast to encase the first, will only last for three days,' Lisle explained when she saw Zoë look at it. 'So we must make haste as we travel through the Library.' She looked again at the covered coffin and added: 'Fortunately our route doesn't involve many stairs.'

'Is it far to your world?' Zoë asked and Lisle shrugged.

'There are several Doors. The one I first discovered is very far away, too much so for us to make that journey. But it's not the only Door that leads to Fenrisnacht. We should reach the nearest in only a few hours.'

Her dog Pepper stood at her feet, looking up with bright-eyed interest at the coffin, and Lisle bent down to pat his woolly head.

'Shall I help with the . . . with Kal?' Jhezra asked and Lisle smiled at her.

'Thank you, but I think perhaps it would be better if

you took the lead. Just along this corridor to begin with and I'll let you know about any changes. Perhaps Zoë can guide the spell casket along and Laura and I will follow behind.'

Laura turned towards Lisle and the older woman lightly touched her arm, turning her to follow after the group.

'Don't worry,' she said. 'I'll let you know if there are any obstacles.'

Morning came quietly to Vespertine Chalcedony's villa. The grey-robed servitors went about their customary routine, opening up the rooms, drawing curtains back from windows and re-lighting lamps in the darker recesses of the house.

Vespertine Chalcedony ate only sparingly and the servants had brought him his usual frugal fare in his rooms. But the villa possessed a grand, if austere, dining room and it was there that the twins went for breakfast. Sitting next to each other at one end of the long table and discussing their plans for the day, they barely noticed the servants silently proffering dishes. But when Morgan arrived they noticed at once.

She was dressed in clothes of the formal style that Vespertine made available to guests. During their years in his service the twins had grown used to this style, although it seemed unique to their patron's private household on Chalice. Vespertine favoured long sweeping robes of silk, unornamented save for a touch of braiding at the wrists or throat. Morgan's gown was of this type, and the silk a shadowy blue like fading bruises. Her long black hair had been combed straight.

She was led into the room by a servant and guided towards the table, the silk gown rustling as she was seated near to the twins. Ciren glanced at Charm and then spoke gently.

'You look better today, Morgan.'

The black-haired girl raised her head slightly but her eyes seemed to take a long time to focus on him.

'I do?' she said and she sounded puzzled. One of the servitors placed a plate of food in front of her and guided her hand towards a fork which she accepted passively, holding it limply in her hand. Ciren wondered if the servants had had to dress her the same way, like a doll, as she stood unprotestingly obedient.

'You should eat,' Charm remarked, watching Morgan narrowly and the girl looked down at the plate without interest.

'I should?' she said and Ciren frowned at the strangeness of her manner.

When they'd taken her from the Converse Court she'd been distraught, clinging to Kal as he begged the Jurists not to send her with the twins. During the journey to Chalice she'd cried openly, frightened by the change in her circumstances. But now she seemed desolate, regarding everything with the same expression of hopelessness.

'Do you fear for Kal?' Ciren asked abruptly. 'The Jurists won't harm him . . .' He stopped as Morgan's empty eyes overflowed and the tears slid down her face before she buried her head in her hands.

A servant stepped forward to move the plate of food away from her and Charm spoke to him.

'Morgan is obviously unwell,' she said. 'There's no point in forcing her to eat.'

The servant bowed and touched Morgan's arm, smoothly helping her out of the seat, an act she accepted with the same hopeless acquiescence.

'Please, don't worry,' Ciren said, feeling Morgan's

misery as if it were his own, and Charm shot a quick glance at him.

'She's clearly not capable of understanding you,' she said, as the servant led Morgan out of the room. 'But it will be different when Vespertine has spoken to her.'

'Will it?' Ciren turned to his twin. 'He wants to use her magic but she's in no state to work spells. She can barely speak. Will he be able to help her?'

'Of course he will.' Charm looked bemused. 'He'll explain the importance of working for the Wheel. Once she's understood that, she won't be so confused.' She paused and then added in harder tones: 'And neither will you.'

'I?' Ciren asked and Charm's black-violet eyes met his. 'You seem concerned for her,' she said coldly. 'You shouldn't be.'

He looked away from her, feeling a flash of annoyance at Charm's decree of what he should or shouldn't be feeling. Morgan was a pitiable figure and he had brought her here. Whenever he looked at her he felt responsible for her state. And yet, he knew that Charm was right, he should have confidence in their patron. It was Vespertine's plans that mattered.

'If she's no use to him, won't we be responsible?' he asked, testingly, and Charm shook her head.

'He'll find a way to make her useful,' she said. 'Magic that powerful should belong to the Wheel. The Jurists would just have wasted that power by sending her home.'

'She didn't want to go back anyway,' Ciren said, remembering the conversations they'd had with Morgan in Shattershard. 'She wanted to be a magician.'

'Yes, of course she did. And she wanted to join the Wheel,' Charm said, approvingly. 'It was Kal who convinced her otherwise. He was too independent for the Wheel. But Morgan will make a useful agent once she's accepted us.'

Charm drained her glass of fruit juice and stood up from the table, seeming satisfied that they were in agreement.

'So,' she said. 'Shall we have that ride then?' She tilted her head at him speculatively. 'If you've finished eating, that is.'

Ciren looked down at his meal, untouched since Morgan had joined them, and felt a sense of revulsion at the congealed food.

'Yes, I'm finished,' he said, standing quickly. 'Let's get out of here.'

A flicker of a frown passed across Charm's face at his vehemence but she turned and led the way out of the room. As they headed for the stables she seemed at ease, coming out of the villa into the misty grey morning sun. But Ciren felt the grey stone walls fall behind him with a burst of relief. As long as Morgan was in the villa he wasn't able to be comfortable there and he tried to hope that Charm was right.

Vespertine would see Morgan and explain things to her and then he wouldn't be troubled by these thoughts he hardly knew how to express.

Alex sagged against the wall, breathing hard, as the rest of the Orientation group pounded past him. He'd already drunk the water in his canteen and he somehow doubted the arms-master would let him take a break to go and get more.

He'd been woken at dawn that morning and had washed in icy cold water before doing his share of cleaning up the barracks. Since then he had run two full circuits of the hilltop encampment and was beginning to think he wouldn't make it round a third. He had a stitch in his side, his uniform was stained with sweat, and he still couldn't get his breath back.

'You!' A voice barked out and Alex involuntarily straightened. Reck, the squad leader, had dropped back and was loping towards him with an easy stride that showed he was having no difficulty with the exercise.

'Squad leader . . .' Alex managed to gasp out, pushing himself away from the wall.

'What's the problem, Salvager?' Reck sneered. 'Can't keep up?'

'Just . . . catching my breath.' Alex gritted his teeth and stumbled back on to the path, at the tail end of the group. He was out of condition. Not that long ago in the desert he would have been able to make this run without needing a break.

'Renegades won't give you time to catch your breath,' Reck snapped. 'Get moving.'

'Sir,' Alex managed to say and pushed his legs into motion despite every muscle complaining at him.

He was still the last of the group but Reck's sneering presence gave him a burst of extra energy, determined not to be shown up.

'Still pitiful,' the squad leader laughed and other cadets glanced back over their shoulders to see who was getting the sharp edge of his tongue. Alex said nothing. For one thing he needed all his breath for the run. For another he knew there was no point arguing. Reck's attitude was typical of this kind of military set-up: his jibes were supposed to be a test.

'You think this is amusing?' Reck demanded, on cue. 'Is this a game to you, Salvager?'

'No, sir.' Alex flicked his eyes sideways and saw Reck's glare.

'Perhaps you need some extra motivation,' Reck

snapped. 'In which case you might like to know that if the Wheel decides you can't be Salvaged you won't just be thrown back to whatever world you crawled out of. The Wheel has no room for failures. Remember that.'

Alex's head snapped up but Reck was already moving forward to join the rest of the group. His feet slamming painfully into the ground, Alex picked up his speed, coming in only a metre behind the last man of the group, as they finished the last circuit of the walls. The others were lining up to refill their flasks from a water pump but Alex didn't join them. His eyes met Reck's and the squad leader glared back at him.

Reck's words had been a warning, one he was lucky to get. Away from Ciren and Charm Alex had forgotten how much danger he was in, how easily the Wheel might decide he was useless. Now he remembered and his thoughts went to Morgan. She must be going through her own version of Salvage. The Wheel wanted her for her magic and they'd already made it clear they would stop at nothing to get it. If they failed, there was no hope for her.

Jhezra thought to herself that they must make a strange sight as they made their way through the winding corridors of the Library. The covered coffin hung in the air between her and Zoë, needing only a gentle push to keep it gliding along smoothly through the air.

But members of the Collegiate were obviously used to magic. Although they gained a few curious glances from people as they passed, they were probably more interested in what the white blanket covered than awed by the fact of it floating in the air. Jhezra herself was relieved that the blanket covered the crystal spell; she found looking at Kal's frozen figure was unpleasant, but once or twice Zoë had lifted the covering and peered through the grey coffin spell.

The route they were taking had led out of Jurist territory and through a Library section that belonged to a faction called the Idolaters.

'They worship books,' Lisle had explained. 'But they think reading them is a sin.'

As a result this area of the Library was the most pleasant Jhezra had seen. The floors were covered in thick soft carpets, and sconces held lamps with coloured shades that shed softly glowing light on the shelves. The books here were placed so that the fronts faced out from the shelves, with long gaps between each one, so that they might be admired in isolation. The covers were richly ornamented in vibrant colours, some with silver or gold or even precious stones inlaid on them.

'Don't try to touch the books,' Lisle warned. 'The Idolaters frown on that as well. Even they only touch them while wearing special gloves.'

'Waste of space,' Laura said when they described the surroundings to her and for a change Zoë agreed with her, keeping to the uneasy truce they had agreed upon.

'Books are *for* reading,' Zoë said. 'They might as well be pictures if no one's going to open them.'

Jhezra thought the books were rather beautiful and she could understand why the Idolaters admired them as they did. The Library was filled with factions with peculiar habits and the Idolaters at least appreciated the books, unlike the Catalogue Cultists with their long lists of where to find even longer lists. She looked with interest at the covers and was rather sorry when the Idolater section came to an end.

The next section was different again. People were hard at work in the rooms that led off the corridor, only sparing a glance for the group as they passed by. The air smelt of burning leather and boiling glue and Jhezra pulled a scarf across her mouth to avoid breathing in too much of the noxious smell.

'Bookbinders,' Lisle said as they hurried past. 'They serve a number of other factions in this area, restoring and manufacturing books.'

Jhezra might have asked to know more but the acrid smell seemed to grow greater every moment as the group hurried on where Lisle led until they came out of the Bookbinder section to an area where the corridor opened up.

The first impression Jhezra got was one of space and for a moment she thought it was another massive room as the Converse Court had been. Then she realized that the place they stood was like the top of a tower, bordered by carved wooden pillars and the spaces between looking out across a great distance to other parts of the Library far beyond.

Coming to the edge Jhezra looked out, holding a wooden pillar for support, and marvelled at what she could see. On the other side of the space she could see the open holes of corridors and spots of black that must be Doors. But in between was a fretwork of blackened and broken wood; a few pieces of walls and floors remaining to show where once a Library section had been.

'What is it?' Laura asked, impatiently. 'Where are we now?'

'This was once the domain of the Woodcarvers,' Lisle said sadly and reached down to pat Pepper's curly head. 'Now it is a wasteland.' Raising her hand she pointed to where the floor sloped down between two pillars and wound in a spiral around a corner and away from the devastation. 'Our route lies that way.'

As Zoë guided the casket and Laura followed carefully

behind, one hand brushing against the solid side of the spiralling path, Jhezra fell into step with Lisle.

'What happened to them?' she asked. 'The Woodcarvers.'

'They kept to the rules while others broke them,' Lisle said, her eyes still scanning the charred and splintered section. 'When I first came to the Library I thought them the wisest of any faction. But within a year I had turned away from them to join the Lightbringers. It wasn't until many years later that I realized how hard it is to deal peace while everyone else threatens war . . .'

Laura's left hand continued to trail along the wooden wall as she walked ahead of them, fingers skating lightly across the figures of people, animals, and trees.

'It sounds as if that's how things work in the Library,' Laura said and turned to add, 'Factions come and seem to prosper, but fail and fall when more powerful groups oppose and overtake them.'

'Yes.' Lisle's expression was bleak as she met the gaze of the blind girl. 'It's a common tale. The exceptions are legends or perhaps myths.'

'What happened to the Lightbringers?' Zoë asked, looking up from the boy spellbound in crystal. 'We heard one of the speakers mention them in the Court and you said you joined them next?'

'The Lightbringers prospered for many years,' Lisle told them. 'But they are long gone now. The Lightbringers were more flexible with the Library laws and people claimed we bent them too far.' She sighed. 'In the end we fell victim to those who bent them so far they broke.'

Lisle looked once more at the broken remains of the Woodcarver section and the charred carvings that could still be made out, crawling crippled and maimed over the splintered wooden walls. Her dog whined softly and the woman sighed, looking away at last to lead them onwards.

The white corridors with their grey curtains and carpets were so similar that it took a while for the realization to penetrate that the servants were not taking her back to the room she had slept in. Holding her arms in a light but firm grip on either side they led Morgan onwards down the corridors to a place where the wall hangings were spidered with the slightest tracery of a pattern. Light and dark blended and swirled in a pattern that wasn't a pattern, making her head swim, and her eyes found it difficult to focus.

One of the servants reached out and pulled the tapestry ahead of them to one side, revealing a door. Then both servants stepped back so that Morgan stood alone before that door.

'Will you enter, lady?' one asked quietly.

'Where is this?' Morgan tried to turn and look back down the corridor, but the servants prevented her, turning her back to face the door.

'Your host awaits you,' the second servant said. 'Will you enter alone or shall we assist you?'

She had no option. Plainly she was expected to go through the door and raising a hand Morgan reached for the handle, and paused. Her hand shook uncertainly and fell on the door, turning her motion into a feeble knock.

'Enter,' a voice said from behind the door and the servants urged her forward again.

One lifted her hand to the handle as the other let the tapestry fall down again over her back. For a moment she was held between the fabric and the wall and she remembered her dream of the night before, the fear of being trapped in cold grey stone. Then the handle turned, the door opened, and she was moving forward, into the room ahead.

The room was grey and the person inside sat in the centre of the dimly lit space. She had seen him in the shadows once before, behind the black and red spoked table of the Wheel. Then his robes had appeared as dark as the room, his face barely visible beneath the hood of his cloak. Now she saw that he wore grey: a dark and dusty grey that seemed strangely darker than the twins' stark and unrelieved black.

'Come closer, child, and stand before me,' Vespertine Chalcedony said and Morgan felt her feet moving forward slowly, bringing her closer to that still figure.

'Yes.' Vespertine's white-rheumed eyes seemed to darken behind the cataracts as he studied her face and Morgan could not meet them.

Instead she stared at the floor. Like everything else in that room it was grey and she felt as if she hung suspended in empty space, with nothing to hold on to anywhere.

'Morgan,' Vespertine said. 'Is that all your name?'

'Morgan Michaels,' she whispered, and wondered why she'd included her surname, something she'd left behind when she left Earth.

'Why did you run away from the Wheel, Morgan?' Vespertine asked, his voice dry and papery, barely making it across the small space that separated them. 'Periphrast Diabasis had high hopes of you.'

'I'm sorry . . .' Morgan's voice failed her and she wetted her lips and tried again. 'Kal . . . Kal said . . .'

It was no good. Just speaking his name summoned the tears and she felt them spill out of her eyes.

'What did he say?' the voice murmured out of the grey haze and somehow the very impersonality made it easier for Morgan to speak.

'That the Wheel would use my magic to conquer worlds . . . that you were breaking the laws of the Library.' The words came out in a rush as she fought back the tears and raised her head to look at the ancient figure in front of her. Repeating Kal's words made her feel closer to him and she gained strength from that.

'He was an intelligent young man. Not many members of the Collegiate have guessed as much,' Vespertine said and Morgan blinked.

'You admit it?' she asked.

'Oh yes, the Wheel does conquer worlds, it's true. But what your young friend could not realize was what those worlds are like.' The old man's lips stretched in a thin smile. 'They are worlds of wonder, Morgan. Sit down, and I will tell you about them.'

Vespertine's was the only chair in the room but the grey carpet was soft and Morgan sat down, crossing her legs beneath her. The old man looked approving, like a benign grandfather, as he started to speak about the Wheel's worlds.

The next few sections Lisle led her small group through seemed uncared for, books covered with dust or cobwebs. Pepper, the dog, sniffed with interest at piles of rubbish left on the floor and Jhezra thought to herself how much the Idolaters would hate to see books left to rot in this shadowy and uncared-for section.

'What faction lives here?' she asked and Lisle sighed.

'Not a faction exactly,' she said. 'The nearby Collegiate members call this the Junkheap. Some people were living here for a while but they seem to have moved on. Perhaps others will come and take their place.'

'Can anyone just take over a section of the Library?' Laura asked and Lisle shrugged.

'More or less,' she said. 'Although some factions do protect their own space quite jealously.'

'Why? Are you thinking of starting your own faction?' Zoë asked with a sneer but Laura's reply was as cool as ever.

'I might,' she said. 'I couldn't be any worse than some of the idiots we've met.' Her voice was amused as she added, 'Glossali Intergrade and his Catalogue Cult, for example.'

'The Catalogue Cult are not very wise,' Jhezra said sharply, feeling for a moment the same sort of irritation with Laura that Zoë displayed. 'But Glossali was kind to us. We shouldn't forget it.'

Laura said nothing and Jhezra swallowed any more harsh words, recollecting that they were always wasted on Laura. Instead she came up to join Zoë where she guided the crystal spell that held Kal's motionless body. The red-headed girl had lifted the covering once more to look at Kal's face.

'Any change?' she asked and Zoë shook her head.

'No . . . no change,' she said and her face was a little flushed as she continued. 'I was just looking because . . . it's like a fairy tale, isn't it?'

'A fairy tale?'

'There's a story called "Snow White",' Zoë explained. 'In it a wicked queen poisons Snow White and these dwarves think she's dead and put her in a crystal casket.' She stroked the white fur covering absent-mindedly and Jhezra had to prompt her to go on.

'Then what happens?' she asked. 'Does Snow White escape?'

'A prince who's riding through the forest finds the casket,' Zoë said, her race reddening again. 'He wakes her with a kiss.'

'It sounds as if you'd like to volunteer to try it.' Laura's voice sounded from behind them and Zoë jumped as if she had been stung.

'Perhaps we should,' Jhezra said thoughtfully. 'I don't know much about magic but surely it couldn't hurt to try?'

Laura laughed quietly behind them and Lisle sounded doubtful as she said, 'I think it's unlikely. But as you say, I don't think it would do any harm.'

Zoë was still blushing fiercely but she managed to say, 'We couldn't try it even if we wanted to. This crystal coffin is solid.'

'And in your story it's a prince who wakes Snow White,' Jhezra said. 'Kal's a prince but perhaps it would need to be a princess to kiss him awake.'

'We could ask Princess Sigrid if she'd be willing,' Lisle said, with a low laugh at what must be some private joke. 'But I don't think she'd appreciate the suggestion.'

Zoë and Jhezra exchanged equally uncomprehending looks but Laura's expression was thoughtful, as if Lisle's comment had meant something more to her.

It was in this shadowy cobwebbed section that Lisle finally told them to stop.

'The Door we want is here,' she explained.

At first Jhezra couldn't see it through the darkness but Lisle pointed out a symbol carved into the corner of a shelf: an animal head with long snout and alert ears. 'See the wolf's head?' Lisle said. 'That's my sign. The Door to Fenrisnacht is around the next corner.'

'Does anyone but you even know it's here?' Laura asked, listening intently to their conversation, and Lisle glanced at her.

'Only a few of my friends,' she said. 'If the Wheel start looking for any of us they'll have trouble finding us here.'

The Door was where Lisle had said it would be and

as they lined up before it Jhezra and Zoë manoeuvred the crystal coffin carefully so that they stood at each end: Jhezra at the front and Zoë at the back. Laura was the first to step through the Door and as she vanished, Lisle moved to follow her, calling Pepper to heel, as she too disappeared into the black void. Then Jhezra took hold of her end of the coffin and stepped backwards through the Door.

Blackness flashed before her eyes and almost simultaneously there was a sharp crack. Zoë appeared before her out of the blackness, still holding her end of the coffin, and they both had to grab at Kal's figure as the crystal coffin simply disintegrated. The spell shattered into thousands of glittering fragments, which fell like rain all around them as they staggered into this new world.

# 5

Zoë stretched out her hand slowly towards the slumped figure of the Archon. She still hadn't got over her fear of the sparkling haze that surrounded him. Spots danced before her eyes and she blinked, trying to clear them, and pressed her fingers to the side of Kal's neck.

There was a fizzing feeling, more a tingle than a jolt, but she jerked back her hand at once. Then, ashamed of herself, she reached out again and felt carefully for a pulse.

'He's alive,' she said after a moment. But his heart-beat seemed strangely slow. She'd taken a first aid course about a year ago and she tried to dredge up what she remembered of it. Kal wasn't exactly human so she couldn't be certain what was normal for him. 'Perhaps we shouldn't move him,' she said uncertainly.

'We must,' Lisle said firmly and Zoë looked up, taking in their surroundings for the first time since they had come through the Door.

They were in a small round room with three stairs leading up to a closed wooden door. The floor was thickly covered with some kind of straw and the room smelt strongly of people and animals. The dog, Pepper, was sniffing around the room in an interested way and Zoë wrinkled her nose, wondering what had inhabited this place before.

'Where are we?' Laura asked, with an edge to her voice, and Lisle glanced over at her.

'This is a way-station about three leagues from the capital of Fenrisnacht. I've sent ahead word for us to be met here and an escort will arrive before too long.' She turned back to Zoë to add: 'We'll take as much care as we can in readying him for travel but we cannot remain here. This place isn't provisioned for a long stay.'

As Zoë did her best to make Kal comfortable, wrapping him with the white fur blanket that had covered the crystal coffin, Jhezra came to kneel next to her at Kal's side.

'The *electric* effect is less than it was,' she said to Zoë, the unfamiliar word sounding strange on her tongue. 'Did you feel it?'

'Yes.' Zoë nodded. 'But why did the crystal spell shatter like that? Do you know?' She looked up at Lisle and the older woman nodded.

'Magic is weaker here,' she said. 'I hoped that either both spells would hold or, more likely, that both would break. But although Tan Ecesis's spell seems to have failed, the one caused by the Archon's crown must still be active.'

'Why don't we try removing it?' Laura asked. She hadn't moved from her position standing against the wall and her expression was thoughtful.

'I don't think we should mess with something we don't understand,' Zoë said pointedly and Jhezra sat back on her heels, looking from her to Laura.

'If nothing else works we might try . . .' she began.

'This is no place for such experiments,' Lisle said firmly. 'Make him as comfortable as you can and I will see if I can spot any sign of our escort.'

The older woman stood, snapping her fingers to call her dog back, and went to the doorway. It was closed firmly with a heavy iron latch and she took hold of the mechanism before looking back at them.

'Shield your eyes,' she said. 'It will be bright outside.'

In Vespertine Chalcedony's study the dim light had faded. Sitting on the floor at his feet Morgan had barely noticed the growing darkness as she listened to the sound of his voice telling her about the worlds the Wheel possessed.

'On the world of Lyoness every building has a bell-tower and when the wind blows they ring with different notes, creating new harmonies with every gust of air.'

'That sounds beautiful,' Morgan said, trying to imagine it.

'The people there value music above everything else. The most respected of the citizens are the composers, but everyone plays some form of instrument and even the children's games are contests not of agility or strength but of singing talent.'

Morgan tried to imagine that, choirs of children instead of football teams, music surrounding you everywhere you went. Vespertine made it sound almost like paradise.

'But before the Wheel came Lyoness was in the middle of a famine. There weren't enough farmers and traders to keep the people fed. Music was all they had. We changed that.'

'How?'

'Through trade with other worlds under our protection. Our agents transport food in huge quantities through the Doors that lead to that world. In return we export musical scores, operas and concertos, even the children's songs . . .'

Vespertine paused for long enough for Morgan to think about it before continuing.

'All our worlds are linked together in this way; organized and harmonious. The Collegiate calls it interference but to each world we bring peace and prosperity. Do you really believe that it's wrong to do so, Morgan?'

'No,' she said slowly. 'But what about Shattershard, the Wheel was helping the Tetrarchate take it over, weren't you?'

'It wasn't us who brought the city down,' Vespertine said softly. 'It was the desert people, the Hajhim, who were resisting the organized plans of the Tetrarchate empire. People are frightened of change, they'll fight to preserve what they call freedom, even if it means freedom to starve, or kill, or die. There's none of that on the Wheel's worlds. We plan everything, every detail, judging what each world and each person needs to make them content. Nothing is ignored, no one is left out of our plans.'

'But they don't have a choice.' Morgan tried to make sense of her own thoughts. Vespertine's calm voice was driving Kal's arguments out of her head but she knew he wouldn't have agreed with what the ancient councillor was saying.

'How much choice do people have on your world?' Vespertine asked her. 'Are people free to do what they want there? Can people lead their lives without fear of being robbed or attacked or hurt?' His voice softened further as he asked, 'What was it you wanted, Morgan, that your world could not give you?'

'I don't know.' Morgan bit her lips and looked down at the pale grey floor. 'I wanted a lot of things.'

'Were you able to use your magic on your own world?' Vespertine asked and she shook her head.

'My world doesn't have magic, or not any that I ever saw,' she told him and then her hands clenched as the bitterness of her life on Earth came back to her. 'If it did, it wouldn't have been so bad. I wouldn't have had to go to a school where everyone thought I was weird, or ride the stupid bus because someone stole my bike.' Her throat closed up and she had to whisper the next words. 'My mum wouldn't have had such a tough time that I got taken into care whenever she couldn't cope.'

Her eyes blurred with tears and she felt a hand descend lightly on her hair, stroking as gently as Vespertine's soothing voice.

'Your life has been hard, I am sure. But it doesn't have to be that way,' he said. 'The Wheel has always wanted to help you, Morgan. My twins saw the possibility in you and valued you for it. That is why we rescued you when the Jurists would have condemned you to return to that world where no one saw your true worth. We will help you more, if you will allow it.'

She still couldn't speak but Vespertine didn't seem to expect an answer.

'I know Kal doesn't trust us, but we'll help him as well. The Jurists separated you but we'll find him for you. Anything you want can be yours, Morgan.'

'Really?' Morgan lifted her tear-stained face to look up at the founder of the Wheel. 'You'll find Kal?'

'I promise,' Vespertine told her and his hand stroked her hair one last time before releasing her. 'Do Ciren and Charm lack for anything? Once you're one of us, no door will be closed to you.'

'What . . . what do I have to do?' Morgan swallowed. 'To be one of you?'

'Only trust us,' he told her. 'Open your heart and your mind to the ways of the Wheel.'

Jhezra had obediently covered her eyes with a hand as the older woman opened the door of the roundhouse. She knew how bright the light reflecting from desert sand could be but the sudden glare that entered the room surprised her all the same. Peering carefully through the net of her fingers she looked up through the open door and tried to make sense of what she saw.

The world outside was white. A great carpet of whiteness lay over the land, rising and falling in undulations like sand dunes but dazzlingly bright in a way that sand could not be. Above, the sky was white too, and if there was a sun up there she couldn't see it because her eyes started to water and she turned her head away.

'White light,' Laura said in a strange voice and Jhezra blinked the tears out of her eyes and turned to look at her. Laura was standing staring out into the strange white world. Her green eyes were held wide open and a frown of concentration creased her forehead.

'You can see it?' Zoë asked. Her own hands were raised to shield her face but Jhezra could hear the doubt in her voice.

'I can see light,' Laura told them. 'Light instead of dark, but that's all.' The excitement in her voice dropped away suddenly as she spoke and Jhezra felt a stab of pity for her.

'That's still good news,' Lisle said, looking back at Laura. 'Remember that magic is weaker here. The curse on you should be weakened as well. But even so you should cover your eyes. Snow-blindness is a danger here.'

Laura nodded, surprisingly obedient for once, and wrapped her green scarf once more across her eyes. Then she rummaged in the bag she carried and took out two more strips of material, the brown scarves she also sometimes used.

'Here,' she said, extending the hand that held them in the direction of the others. 'You can borrow these if you want.'

'My thanks,' Jhezra said, standing and taking them. It was the first time in a long while that Laura had made such a gesture. Giving one to Zoë she wrapped the other across her own eyes and squinted through the loose weave of the material.

'Thank you,' Zoë said a moment later, suspicious as always of Laura.

Lisle had already shielded her face and was standing outside the entrance, turning her head to look around. Jhezra came to join her and tried to make sense of the scenery. There were rocks and trees scattered around the bleak landscape, each lightly dusted with whiteness, but distance was almost impossible to judge.

'What *is* this?' Jhezra asked and, coming to stand next to her, it was Zoë who answered.

'It's snow,' she said and suddenly shivered. 'And it's really cold.'

Jhezra had noticed that since they first arrived. A bone-chilling cold that seemed to penetrate her clothing as if it were muslin. But everywhere seemed cold to her in comparison to her home world.

'Snow like Snow White?' she asked, understanding now the name in the story.

'Yes.' Zoë nodded. 'Because her skin was as white as snow.' This time when she said the words Jhezra heard the meaning behind them and she touched her translation amulet lightly, wondering again how its magic could convey the sense of another language.

'Fenrisnacht must be the opposite of your own world,' Lisle said, smiling at her. 'You have desert and sand. We have tundra and snow. But I imagine some of the same rules apply to both. If you ever find yourself lost, beware of exhaustion that makes you want to sleep. To sleep in the snow is death.'

'I understand,' Jhezra said seriously. She smiled back at the woman, recognizing an affinity that the two of them shared, before looking back at the strange landscape. 'It's beautiful,' she said softly.

'Yes,' Lisle said quietly. 'It is.'

They stared out at the snow-covered land for a moment more. Then Lisle stepped back.

'We're losing heat by keeping the door open,' she said. 'The escort will let us know when they arrive. For now we should conserve as much warmth as we can while we wait.'

'So who is this escort?' Laura asked as Jhezra and Zoë helped heave the heavy door back into place. 'Can you be sure they'll arrive before we freeze to death?'

'If they don't we can step back though the Door,' Lisle pointed out with a dry smile, turning to indicate the black void in the wall through which they had entered. 'But I think they'll come soon. This way-station is on the regular route of the queen's Wolves and my youngest daughter is their captain.'

As she spoke Lisle bent down and rummaged in the thick straw piled at the side of the room before unearthing a small wooden chest and opening it. Pepper whined quietly and Lisle reached out absent-mindedly to ruffle the dog's silky ears as she took out a couple of wrapped packages from the chest.

'There are some provisions here,' she said. 'Dried meat

and fruit, if you're hungry.' Taking out a large leather bottle she added, 'And this is glorwin, it's warming.'

'My thanks,' Jhezra said, accepting the bottle and carefully levering out the stopper. The drink smelt of spice and spirits and she took a small sip and felt the warmth of the drink slide down her throat and hit her stomach with a sudden glow. 'It's good,' she said, appreciatively, handing the bottle on.

'Tell us more about the people who are coming here,' Laura said, uninterested in the refreshments. Her hands fiddled with a few strands of straw, plaiting them between her fingers, in an unusual sign of restlessness. 'Since we're going to be meeting them any moment.'

'The Wolves are the army of Fenrisnacht,' Lisle explained, as she unwrapped some dried strips of meat and fed the dog from her hand. 'Also the closest thing we have to a messenger system. They travel between the baronies in small bands, making sure that people hold to the queen's laws.'

'You said your daughter led them,' Zoë said, interestedly. 'Do you have many children?'

'Three.' Lisle smiled slightly, her eyes distant. 'Meaga is the eldest. She runs my estate in the Hinterland. She and her husband have four children of their own; that makes me feel old.' Her mouth twisted wryly before continuing. 'Lechto is my son, he's married now as well and lives away from home. Siffany is the one I spoke of, captain of the Wolves, she reports directly to the queen.'

'Which is most like you?' Jhezra asked curiously and Lisle gave her a narrow look.

'Probably Lechto,' she said and there was something grim in her expression as she added, 'He's the most rebellious.'

Jhezra and Zoë grinned at her but Laura frowned. Her voice was impatient as she interrupted them.

'So the Wolves enforce the queen's laws. Who is the queen?'

Lisle paused before answering and Zoë looked annoyed at the other girl's brusqueness, but Jhezra reminded herself that she had asked for Laura's help. Laura was good at seeing the way the worlds worked and her questions were never trivial.

'Her name is Lachesis,' Lisle said slowly. 'She is the niece of Wutan, who was king before her, and she came to power about thirty years ago. She's the most enlightened ruler Fenrisnacht has had in centuries . . . and a personal friend of mine.'

'I see,' Laura said, with a touch of irony, and Jhezra wondered what it was she had understood. It wasn't that she didn't trust Lisle; she liked the older woman who had helped them more than once, but she suspected Laura would be the first to spot any sign of betrayal.

'I brought you through this Door because it's the most convenient for the Jurist section of the Library,' Lisle was explaining. 'It's also the nearest to the capital and the royal palace. But there are more Doors from Fenrisnacht that lead to other worlds or different sections of the Library. Once you've had a chance to get your bearings we can talk about what you want to do next.'

'Is there likely to be anyone here who can cure Kal?' Zoë asked, turning back to the sleeping figure enveloped by the white blanket. 'Or Laura, for that matter,' she added.

'Not cure,' Lisle said. 'Although both spells have been weakened. But the Library is vast, as you know, and there are sections that are very different from the ones you've seen so far. There are people I know of who may be able to help.'

Laura was about to speak again but suddenly Lisle raised a hand to shush her.

'Can you hear something?' she asked.

Zoë listened and then shook her head but Jhezra kept listening. The wind must have increased outside the roundhouse though because she could hear it rushing and whistling around the walls. Then she heard another note and cocked her head, listening harder.

'I hear it,' Laura said. 'A horn call.'

'That was it.' Lisle nodded, getting to her feet again, and Jhezra hastened to help her open the door.

Pepper nosed past their feet to join them at the entrance and Lisle lifted her arm to point across the snow.

'There,' she said. 'See, by the tree line.'

In the distance a line of black was snaking its way across the snow, heading towards them at what Jhezra guessed must be considerable speed. A low humming note sounded again and she realized that must be the horn call which she had previously mistaken for one of the wind's noises.

Jhezra narrowed her eyes and squinted through the scarf and the cold wind to try to see the approaching escort. But although she thought she could see the figures of people they were lost in a confusion of unfamiliar shapes and a flurry of movement, all coming together at speed, skimming over the snow faster than she could have thought possible.

'Yes,' Lisle said, her voice gaining strength. 'The Wolves are coming.'

The landscape of Chalice had been tamed. Riding out from the villa, Charm and Ciren headed along a familiar route down the smooth grey road into the countryside. Chalice was a triumph of Vespertine Chalcedony's talents for organization. None of the Wheel's other worlds had reached this level of control but Vespertine had held Chalice for longer than any other of their possessions and it showed. The twins had often been taken out on this route by carriage, as Vespertine showed them some of his principles of management and promised them worlds like this of their own some day.

As they rode they overtook several wagons, each marked with a sign or glyph depicting their cargo and point of origin, drawn by the same breed of stocky shire-horse. A broad bridge crossed a waterway where similarly marked barges passed underneath. In the fields to either side men and women worked methodically, tilling the land and tending to the crops.

At a crossroads, Charm reined in to look across at her twin. Ciren's face had brightened on leaving the villa and the ride looked as if it was beginning to blow some of the cobwebs out of his head and she looked at him quizzically.

'Which route shall we take?' she asked. 'To the hill fort to see the soldiers training? Or towards the mines or down to the fishing village, perhaps?'

'What about off the road?' Ciren asked and Charm frowned, looking to the left where the farms ended and a wooded area began, separated off from each other and from the road by a low railed fence.

'I don't think there's anything to see,' she said doubtfully, wondering if her twin was entirely well.

'No, but let's try it anyway,' he said, with a sudden smile that dispelled her doubts. Backing his mount, he aimed at the fence and kicked it into a run. The tall grey stallion, bred for speed and agility, bunched its muscles and cleared the fence in an easy jump before cantering on between the trees. 'Are you coming?' Ciren turned to call and Charm wheeled her own horse.

The grey mare leapt the fence as easily as her brother's horse had and Charm followed Ciren between the trees. She didn't know what her twin had been expecting but she hoped he wouldn't be disappointed. This was a managed forest, planted, coppiced, and felled by Vespertine's people, the trees evenly spaced and of the same few basic types. Even the leaf mulch hadn't built up under the trees, but was removed and used as fertilizer for the fields.

As they rode up the easy undulation of the land, Charm wondered if it would be long before Vespertine sent them out on another mission. Chalice was peaceful but somehow the peace didn't suit her as well as exploring the landscapes of other worlds or the galleries of the Library. Her twin never seemed to have these questions of identity when they were travelling. At least, Charm didn't think so. Now that she considered it, her memories of the last mission were oddly indistinct. Ciren had been acting strangely then, she recalled, but Vespertine had dealt with the problem.

Her musing was interrupted when Ciren called from ahead and she looked up to see they had reached the edge of the tree line and she reined in her horse as they came out on a grass bank by the side of a lake. It was broad and flat, stretching from the forest to a rocky shore on the far side, reflecting the blue-grey sky in a still mirror.

But it wasn't a perfect mirror. After a moment Charm saw that the surface of the lake was covered with a trailing mat of greenery which crawled down the rocky slopes and had stretched out long streamers of vines across the surface of the water. Here and there a few gaps in the hyacinthine leaves showed the roots floating underneath the lake, coiling around and about each other.

'Have you been here before?' Ciren asked, and Charm shook her head.

'No,' she said. 'But this must be the reservoir, it supplies clean water to the settlements downhill.'

'Perhaps the plant helps to filter the water.' Ciren stared down at the plant tendrils that choked the lake and added, 'No fish, though.'

'I suppose they would make the water less clean.' Charm shrugged. 'Besides, the fishing villages are three miles to the east. There's no need to have fish here as well.' She nudged her horse along the side of the lake and cocked her head at her twin. 'I hope you're not planning to go swimming,' she said.

He was slow to meet her eyes and when he did his expression was troubled again but he set his horse after hers.

'Is that why we never came here as children?' he asked her. 'Because we couldn't swim in the lake?'

'I don't remember.' Charm was puzzled by the question. 'It makes sense though. There really isn't anything much to do here, except ride.'

'We could have climbed the trees,' Ciren suggested.

'But we didn't,' she said, wondering why he would want to. 'Did we?'

'I can't remember,' her twin said quietly.

Laura could hear the escort's approach across the snow. A slooshing sound and a flurry of motion coming closer; it carried with it the smell of animals and people. Then the noise slid to a halt and was replaced by people calling out greetings, intermingled with panting animals and whines and yips from around her feet.

Sleighs, Laura decided. This escort must have come by sleigh and feeling furry bodies pressing up against her legs she realized that 'Wolves' might not be a metaphor. Despite herself, she stepped back into the shelter of the doorway. Being surrounded by so many people made her blindness more of a handicap and she held on to the rough walls of the roundhouse for balance.

'Mother,' a confident voice rang out and Lisle's voice replied.

'I didn't think you would come yourself, Siffany. Or has Lachesis demoted you to leading patrols.'

'Not yet,' the unfamiliar voice laughed merrily before continuing. 'But how could you doubt I would come? Especially when your letter sent such dire warning.'

'That news can keep until we reach court,' Lisle said, quellingly. 'And we should make haste. My young companions here are not used to such cold and one inside is unwell and must be brought quickly into better shelter than this.'

'Of course.' Siffany accepted Lisle's rebuke without rancour and her voice could be heard ordering her troop to reassemble. Laura jumped as someone slung a warm cloak around her shoulders.

'Mount up, young lady,' someone said, taking her arm. 'There'll be a blizzard before nightfall.'

Laura flinched at the rough handling and it was with a feeling of relief that she heard Jhezra's voice interpose itself.

'Laura is blind,' she said. 'I will help her,' and a gentler arm guided her forwards.

'Thank you,' Laura said out loud, trying to assert herself. But in the surrounding confusion it was hard to tell what was going on.

'It is a carriage pulled by dogs,' Jhezra was saying as she helped Laura into a curved seat, before adjusting the cloak around her. 'There are five of them and we are in the second. The soldiers are carrying Kal to one of the other carriages and Lisle is with Zoë in the first . . . Are you comfortable enough?'

'I'm fine,' Laura said quickly. 'How many soldiers are there in this escort?'

'Perhaps twenty all told,' Jhezra said, keeping up her explanation as she settled herself next to Laura. 'They have closed up the door of the roundhouse and the dogs are forming up in the traces again. The first carriage looks ready to depart.'

There was a jingle of harness and a sudden barking and then Laura felt the sleigh pull forward with a jerk and a whish of sound. Then they were skimming smoothly across the snow and she heard Jhezra laugh with pleasure.

'This is incredible,' the Hajhi girl said and Laura suppressed a smile.

'The kind of vehicle you describe is called a sleigh,' she murmured. 'We have them in the colder parts of my world.' She paused to pull the hood of the cloak up around her head; the wind was bitingly cold and she could feel flakes of snow settling on her face. 'Tell me, are these dogs large and grey?'

'They are large,' Jhezra said, raising her voice to be heard over the sound of their passage. 'But not grey. They are as white as the snow. The escort soldiers wear white fur and leather, I could not see them until they were almost at the roundhouse.'

'Camouflage,' Laura said softly, leaning into Jhezra so she would not have to shout. 'Like the robes the Hajhi wear in the desert. And the dogs are wolves. Fierce animals, not easily tamed.'

'What does that mean to you?' Jhezra asked, her own voice quietened, and Laura shrugged.

'That this world is not tamed,' she said. 'There are more dangers here than the snow.'

'That's not all.' Jhezra was whispering now. 'You learnt something from what Lisle said before, or guessed something I did not. What was it?'

'It was only a thought,' Laura said. 'I'll let you know when I am certain.'

'Very well.' Jhezra leaned away again.

Laura smiled within the warmth of her furred cloak. Jhezra was more observant than she'd expected and she was right. Lisle had told them little enough but there were a couple of things she'd given away, such as the fact that she had power and influence in this world and in the Library. Laura was willing to bet that this 'enlightened' Lachesis had not gained the throne quite as easily as Lisle would have them believe. There were complicated politics in operation here and if there was something Laura was good at it was unravelling the threads of power.

As whiteness blurred across her eyes Laura decided the older woman had been right. This was a good place for a fresh start.

# 6

Not for the first time, Zoë was finding the reality of another world very different from how she might have imagined it. The sleighs travelled swiftly through the white landscape and all she could make out was the occasional round dome-like building through the swirling flakes of snow.

It was cold and she was glad of the warmth of her coat as well as the piles of fur that were heaped in the sleigh. Back on Earth Zoë would never have dreamed of wearing fur but here she didn't object and surreptitiously stroked the soft white pelt of the blanket Lisle's daughter had thrown over their knees. The dogs that pulled the sleigh were huge and white, and with long snouts that made them look wolfish. Zoë had only seen wolves in zoos but, looking at the sleigh-dogs now, she thought these animals were more like wolves than the real thing.

She thought that the dogs couldn't actually *be* wild, because they drew the sleighs. But all the same she had dodged away from their seething bodies when the escort arrived. Pepper, Lisle's dog, seemed similarly nervous and now was bundled up with them in the back of the sleigh under Lisle's knees and all that could be seen of him was a reddish pair of ears peaking out from the blanket.

'He's confused,' Lisle had called out over the noise of their travelling when she saw Zoë looking. 'He was bred here but the cold still comes as a shock.' The older woman herself looked exhilarated, her cheeks and nose were pink but she kept leaning forward to call out questions to her daughter about people and places Zoë didn't know.

Twisting back in her seat, Zoë tried to make out the people in the other sleighs but the blizzard made it impossible. Jhezra was looking after Laura; she seemed to have taken over the task completely and Zoë felt a stab of guilt over how difficult she still found it to deal with her ex-friend. The escort had lifted Kal's body carefully into a sleigh and swaddled him with furs but Zoë couldn't help thinking once more how vulnerable the young Archon was in his spelled state.

'Don't worry,' Lisle said, touching Zoë's knee gently. 'Your friends will be fine. The Wolves won't let harm come to them and we'll be at the palace soon.'

'The palace . . .' Zoë said and Lisle smiled at her.

She tried to imagine what the palace would be like and came up with a crystalline version of the Shattershard fortress with glittering turrets of ice; the kind of palace the Snow Queen had to imprison people in the fairytale. The city, when they came to it, took her by surprise. It appeared quite suddenly when they passed through a gap between two high hills on either side, rising out of the valley beyond. Zoë sat up with a start as the wind whipped away a gust of snow and she saw what looked almost like a city back home: tower blocks rising up from the snow-laden ground.

As the sleighs skimmed closer and Zoë peered at the buildings the resemblance decreased. The tower blocks were only a few storeys high: the lower levels built of stone and the higher ones of wood. There were a few windows, all of which were closed with heavy iron or wooden shutters, and a few doors, some appearing on higher levels, connected by wooden walkways on heavy iron-bound posts.

As the sleighs raced up a central street the city closed in around them and Zoë saw glimpses of stables and animal shelters in the base levels of the buildings. Through the posts she saw a few hurrying figures shadowed by the walkways above and at one point they passed a man feeding a pack of dogs, throwing them haunches of meat. The sleigh slackened for a moment before its driver flicked a whip warningly over the animals in the traces.

The palace itself was like any of the other buildings, although it was the largest by some way. The sleighs pulled up and Zoë found herself being bundled out as quickly as she had been bundled in and Lisle took her arm as they were rushed under a walkway and into a ground-level opening. It was long, like a stable, but the stalls were kennels for dogs. A staircase of stone with thick wooden banisters led up from one corner and Lisle guided her towards it, following her daughter.

'The others?' Zoë said, with a feeling of alarm, and Siffany turned to give her a smile. 'They're right behind you,' she said. 'Just come up here and you can catch your breath.'

Zoë hesitated for another moment and heard Jhezra's voice behind her.

'We're here, Zoë,' she said and as Zoë started up the

stairs she could half see the Hajhi girl's dark-brown eyes meeting hers through a blur of fur-cloaked people.

Then they were climbing the steps and already Zoë could feel the temperature changing before they came up into another large room where iron braziers were burning brightly in the corners and iron lanterns hung on chains from the stone ceiling.

Siffany threw her white cloak on to a stout wooden bench and turned to help Lisle out of her own cloak with an easy affection that made Zoë realize the young woman was really fond of her mother. Lisle sat down for a moment on the bench to shake the snow from her boots and give Pepper a pat of reassurance and Siffany turned to Zoë.

'You should take off your cloaks,' she said, and added, 'or outer garments. Now that we are inside they will be stealing warmth instead of giving it.'

'I'll take yours, Laura,' Jhezra said, shucking her own cloak at once, and Zoë began to take her coat off.

'I'll carry it with me,' Zoë said firmly when Siffany moved to take it from her. 'I don't want to lose it.'

The twins rode around the edge of the lake and Ciren looked out across the blue-green water, not seeing it. On the other side the vines crawling over rock gave way to jagged crags, like a row of teeth. High up on the range, a round tower rose out of the rocks, plain and unfortified. Looking that high made Ciren feel dizzy but his eyes kept travelling back to it, picking at it like a half-healed wound.

The same sense of dislocation that had come over him the previous night was back. Chalice was the closest place to a home he possessed, Vespertine was his patron, and Charm his constant companion. But when he tried to remember growing up here he drew a blank. He knew there had been lessons, training in swordcraft and bowmanship, books of strategy and scholarly treatises, long discussions with his patron that lasted into the night. But all of it seemed strangely distant. Travelling the worlds was his reality and the beginning of those travels was lost in a mist.

'Do you remember us being children at all?' he asked.

Charm gave him a long look and then her face twitched and she shook her head as if troubled by a fly or gnat. But there were no small insects like that here.

'Haven't you asked me that before?' she said. Then she went on before giving him time to reply. 'No, I remember very little. We studied, we trained, we visited the worlds of the Wheel. It was then much as it is now. Except we were more under our patron's guidance.'

'Think back,' Ciren pressed her. 'Do you remember anything from when we were very young? A nurse who looked after us, toys we had, do you remember playing at all?'

'Playing?' Charm's eyes sparked with something that might have been irritation. 'We were given worlds to play with, twin. What do you want, a spinning top? A bat or a ball, perhaps?'

'No. Just a memory of having a childhood,' Ciren said.

'Perhaps I should read your mind and look for one,' Charm said with an edge of sarcasm and Ciren stiffened.

'Why do you say that?' he asked, turning to his twin with a sudden dread. 'You've never read my mind . . . have you?'

He felt suddenly queasy, as if the grey sky was pressing on him, weighing him down, and he slipped from the saddle to stand on the springy turf and lean against the warm flank of the stallion.

'Ciren?' His twin's voice sounded with sudden alarm but as she came quickly to his side he flinched back from her. 'What's wrong?' she asked.

The world spun and he sank to his knees, finding it hard to breathe. The far rock walls of the distant shore stretched and expanded and closed in again and the distant tower wheeled, pinning the earth to the sky. The tendrils of water-hyacinth reached out to drag at him and his magical sense thundered in his head. He could feel Charm's magic close by like a black wheel threatening to suck him in and devour him.

'You've never read my . . . my mind,' he stammered out still holding himself away from that threatening force.

'No . . . I haven't,' Charm said but her voice came distantly and like the rest of the world it was dizzyingly wrong.

'But . . . you have.' His eyes fixed on hers with a sudden horror. 'I remember now. You have.'

Black-purple eyes stared into his, twin tunnels into that roiling dark whirlpool of power. Ciren knew now that he was afraid of that power, had always been afraid of it being used against him as his twin had used it against so many of their victims.

Jhezra had never entered Shattershard's palace but she had heard it was full of wealth that should have belonged to the tribes. Precious metals and jewels covered even the walls, she had been told, and the windows were pictures in coloured glass. Fenrisnacht's palace was not like that but it seemed wealthy enough to her eyes. She thought, privately, that if the Hajhi had taken over Shattershard's palace it might have been a bit like this.

The rooms were large and plain, but she didn't feel the bite of the cold. Heat came from the iron braziers or fireplaces built into the walls. After the bottom level where straw had been piled up on the floor as it had been in the roundhouse, they had been taken up two more of stone, the first with floor coverings of dyed hides and the second with thick rugs of fur. Finally they were led up to a level where the walls were wood and bedrooms opened off a long corridor a little like the way rooms occurred in the Library.

Two men had carried Kal up the stairs ahead of them and taken him into one of the bedrooms. Zoë followed the men carrying Kal, obviously concerned to see that he was safe. Meanwhile, one of the people who had accompanied them through the palace opened a door to another bedroom and ushered Jhezra and Laura inside.

'You can use this room while you wait to see the queen,' the stranger said, in a tone that assumed no possibility of disagreement, and left them there.

The room was plainly appointed and contained one large bed piled high with furs, a small washing stand and a tall cupboard with a mirror bolted to one of the doors. Jhezra dropped her pack on the bed and turned to look at Laura.

'I can guess it's a bedroom,' Laura said snidely and Jhezra bit her tongue to stop herself getting annoyed. She had already realized that snide comments were one of the ways Laura deflected attention from what she was really thinking.

'I wasn't going to waste time describing it,' Jhezra said. 'We may not have long before they call us to speak to the queen. What I want to know is what you think of this place.'

Laura said nothing and Jhezra moved around the bed

to look at herself in the mirror and run her fingers through her hair to tidy it somewhat. It was a small bit of discourtesy that she would not have performed in the presence of another blind person but it relieved her feelings of annoyance with Laura a bit.

'We have an agreement,' she reminded Laura. 'And even if your thoughts so far are only guesses, I would still like to hear them.' She paused and then said carefully, 'Otherwise I will not share with you some descriptive details about this place that *would* interest you.'

'All right.' Laura felt her way to the edge of the bed and sat down. 'But tell me something first . . . is there a window in this room?'

'One that is shuttered.' Jhezra turned and saw Laura carefully removing her blindfold and wondered if it was a ploy to deflect her attention. But she couldn't preserve her coldness completely and asked, 'What do you see?'

Laura's apple-green eyes blinked once and watered and Laura wiped at them with the scarf and blinked some more.

'It's blurry,' she said after a moment. 'Brown, white, some shapes.' Her voice sharpened with a sudden irritation that Jhezra was sure could be no act. 'Nothing I can make out.'

'It has been . . .' Jhezra paused, trying to think, 'ten days, or something more, since you could last see. Perhaps it will take your eyes some time to adjust.'

'Yes, well, I've heard that before.'

Jhezra resisted the urge to say something consoling. Instead she asked, 'Would you like me to tell you what I've noticed?'

'Yes, and then I'll tell you what I suspect,' Laura said agreeably.

Jhezra eyed her suspiciously, not really wanting to

give away an advantage, but it wasn't as if she had learned very much.

'What I think,' she explained, 'is that this is a military kind of building. It's not obvious because these people seem to be at peace, at the moment. But each level is connected to the one below it at only a couple of points, by a staircase or a ladder, and each opening can be closed from the level above. There are trapdoors and heavy iron hasps, which could be used to bar them if they were shut. The walkways we saw outside have stout pillars supporting them but the crossways planks could be detached, turning each building into a separate tower.'

'You're saying that this place is built for defence,' Laura summarized and Jhezra nodded, before she remembered Laura couldn't see her.

'Yes, and in war, a defensible camp is a strong advantage.'

'I remember,' Laura said and Jhezra had a memory of similar conversations back in Shattershard with Laura and Alex plotting how to bring the city down.

'Unlike Shattershard this is no fortress,' she pointed out. 'But the people here are used to war.'

Laura sat silently for a moment, processing, and just as Jhezra wondered if she intended to speak she said thoughtfully, 'That meshes with what I guess.' She paused and then began in a slightly lecturing tone. 'Lisle described the queen as the most enlightened ruler this world had had for centuries. She also said she was the *niece* of the previous king and had come to power about thirty years ago. What she didn't say was that Lachesis inherited the throne naturally.'

'Did she not?' Jhezra tried to think back but couldn't remember much of the conversation. However Laura seemed certain.

'Ruling families pass the throne down to their heirs. There might be some innocent reason why Lachesis inherited the throne from her uncle. But I suspect that's not what happened.'

'You think she stole the throne?' Jhezra asked incredulously.

'Yes, and I think Lisle helped her do it,' Laura said, seemingly suddenly eager to impress Jhezra with her certainty rather than dismissing her ideas as guesses. 'Lisle isn't just some old granny. She's a powerful woman who has her own estate. She's a personal friend of the queen and her daughter is the general of the *army*!'

Laura laughed then and turned her head towards Jhezra, narrowing her eyes as she tried to see her.

'She's no better than us,' she said. 'Lisle came from Fenrisnacht into the Library and met up with the factions she told us about. Then she used her knowledge of other worlds to do what we tried to do in Shattershard. The only difference is that she succeeded.'

Alex lay on his bed in the barracks, trying to relax. Most of the squad were at lunch, taking advantage of the first real break of the day. But he needed to think more than he needed to eat. A few other squad members were checking over their kit or making notes in their books but none of them had spoken to him and Alex hadn't attempted to approach them either.

He was beginning to see what his life might be like as a member of the Wheel. The early morning drill had been followed by two hours of weapons training, a class on survival skills, and an hour's 'orientation' with a dour-faced woman who had lectured him at length on what the Wheel expected of its agents. The emphasis had been on obedience more than anything else. *I never thought of myself as a follower,* Alex thought. *But the Wheel doesn't seem to have a use for me as anything else.*

His particular skills simply weren't that unusual. He thought he'd acquitted himself creditably in front of the armsmaster when he'd shown that he actually could use a sword. But it had quickly become clear that at least half the squad was as good or better than he was with the sabres they were training with and when they'd moved over to other weapons he'd failed dismally with both the thin foil and the heavy hand-and-a-half sword they'd tried him with. When the rest of the squad had moved on to archery he'd had to spend half an hour trying to learn the correct stance and practising drawing a bow. The armsmaster hadn't let him loose a single arrow by the time training was over.

Survival skills class had been equally frustrating. The instructor fired off problems at the squad and the others had rattled off replies with military precision, each one making it plain that he had visited any number of worlds and read about military engagements in many more. At the end of the class Alex had been told to spend an extra hour a day working in the fort library reading up on 'elementary texts'. Still the day wasn't even half over and he had yet to attend classes in tool construction, field medicine, and language skills. Somehow he doubted he'd have much chance to shine at any of those.

If the point had been to show him how much he still had to learn, then he'd taken it. But when he considered days, weeks, and months of this stretching out in front of him, he felt a surge of resentment. After all, he'd never asked for this. In the Library people had been too busy criticizing him and dictating punishments to bother warning him that a faction might kidnap him like this. He would have been better off being sent back to Earth; at least there he knew where the nearest Door was, and it wasn't guarded by a group of cold-blooded soldiers armed to the teeth.

Or it wasn't yet. After all, conquering worlds seemed to be the basis of what the Wheel did and he rather suspected Earth was on their list. Why else had the Salvage instructor told him to write notes on his own world and the location of its Doors?

Alex shifted uncomfortably on the hard mattress. No one even expected him to object, that was the thing that really got to him. He was supposed to go along with all this like a good little Salvager and maybe, if he was loyal enough, the Wheel might someday entrust him with even more of their dirty work. He might not exactly have been a bleeding-heart liberal in Shattershard but this was a bit much. What had the Wheel done for him that he should casually hand over plans for them conquering Earth?

Somehow he didn't doubt that they could do it. The Wheel had everything on their side: weapons, magic, and some of the most heartless bastards he'd ever met. Really the only question he had was whether there was any point even trying to object.

After they were shown upstairs at the palace, the queen's surgeon arrived to look at Kal. Zoë doubted he'd be able to help with a magical problem but she didn't have the opportunity to ask about it. Instead she was shown into a bedroom near by. She'd barely had time to splash some water on her face and rake a brush through her hair when Lisle showed up.

'I hope you haven't been feeling abandoned,' she said as she came in.

'No, that's OK.' Zoë noticed that the older woman's dog wasn't at her heels and she asked: 'Where's Pepper?'

'Oh, I asked the kennel master to look after him. There are a few others of the same breed here. He'll enjoy himself running around with them while we're here.'

'You don't plan to stay long?' Zoë said and Lisle shook her head.

'This is just the first stage of my journey,' she explained. 'I plan to travel onwards to a world called Mandarel. But I must cross Fenrisnacht to get to a Library Door that will take me there.'

'I thought you said the Library wasn't safe any more,' Zoë said doubtfully.

'The Jurist section is not,' Lisle said carefully. 'But not all of the Library is like the parts you've seen.'

'Well, none of the parts we've seen have been like each other,' Zoë pointed out and her companion smiled.

'True enough, but the place I plan to travel to is different again. More . . . enlightened. Less stultified by rules and codes. On the world of Mandarel is a city with ten Doors, each leading into a different part of the Library. Those who live there call it the Mandela and it's a centre of scholarship. Mandarel can defend itself from any Library faction, even the Wheel, and the people there might well be able to help Kal.'

'I see,' Zoë said and Lisle added:

'Also it's the home of the friend who warned me about the Wheel in the first place. Caravaggion.'

'The friend of Dynan, the blacksmith in the village, the person who thinks it's useless to give anyone advice.' Zoë was surprised by how sharp the words sounded in her mouth, as if they had come from Laura, and she ducked her head.

'Yes, he can be inclined to epigrams,' Lisle said, not sounding offended. 'But when he does give advice it tends to be useful and he knows more about the worlds than anyone else I know or have ever heard of.'

Zoë thought about it and then sighed, stroking the fabric of her leather coat lying on the bed next to her. Everything just seemed to lead her further and further away from home.

'Of course, you are free to travel where you will,' Lisle said, as if reading her thoughts. 'But remember that the Wheel now have a route back to your own world, the one they claimed they would use to return Alex and Morgan, according to the Jurist verdict. Caravaggion warned me that the Wheel are empire-builders. If your world seems valuable to them, they may try to use it for their advantage.'

'That sounds like something from a book called *The Lord of the Rings*,' Zoë said, speaking more to herself than Lisle. 'When they get back to Hobbiton it's been taken over by evil.'

'Well, it might not be as bad as that . . .' Lisle said. 'But remember the rules against you telling people from your own world about Doors. If you wish to stop the Wheel you must do so yourself or seek the help of other members of the Collegiate.'

'But there's nothing I can do to stop them,' Zoë protested. 'I don't have magic powers, I can't fight, I can't even stop Laura trying to take over every place we come to . . . I'd be crazy to try and stop the Wheel doing anything.'

'At least you know something about them,' Lisle said. 'And you know Morgan. It may be that the Wheel intend to use her as a weapon.'

'Those *agents* said they'd take her back to Earth,' Zoë said, swallowing. 'But I didn't believe them.'

'As you've discovered, the Great Library is very flawed,' Lisle said, and her voice was sad. 'Those of us who live in the worlds must decide by our own lights how to preserve what we care for.'

# 7

If there was a way in which being blind was useful, it was that it forced you to imagine what strangers were like on the basis of their voices. Laura had built up a picture of people she'd met like Glossali Intergrade or the Jurist leaders that might not mesh exactly with reality but she was convinced she'd be able to recognize her own ideas in them.

She hadn't had much time to evaluate the people they'd met so far in Fenrisnacht and when they were eventually brought in to meet the queen she listened intently to their introduction.

'These are the visitors who came with Lisle,' a firm female voice said as they entered and Laura recognized it as belonging to Siffany. It wasn't hard to imagine an image of Lisle's daughter. An older, Nordic-looking version of Jhezra was how Laura saw her; fair skinned with ice-blue eyes.

'Their names are Zoë, Jhezra, and Laura,' Lisle

explained, as they came forward. 'The fourth, the young man named Kal, is yet unconscious.'

'I bid you welcome to the Winter Palace,' a new voice spoke. 'I am Lachesis, the Wolfshead Queen.'

It was a frosty voice, cold and brittle, words clipped off short so that each one stood out from the next. As the others murmured various polite words of greeting Laura recalled paintings of Elizabeth I during the middle of her reign, substituting a fur-collared cloak for the traditional pleated ruff.

'Come and sit here,' the queen said and Laura felt Jhezra guide her to a seat. She could feel the heat from a fire near by, warming her on one side, and turning towards it the darkness of the room lifted and orange-gold light twisted and flickered about the edges of her eyes.

'You're very kind,' Zoë was saying shyly and Laura fought her own annoyance. It seemed that the red-haired girl was simply unable to match her behaviour to the milieu they found themselves in. She was the same to everyone and considered any attempt at discretion as devious.

'What do you think of my palace?' the queen was asking and this time it was Jhezra who answered.

'It is pleasant,' she said. 'Impressive but not luxurious.'

'Not *luxurious*?' The queen's words were satirical but Laura thought she could detect a note of approval in her voice.

'Perhaps my words don't translate very well,' Jhezra said carefully and Laura thought to herself that the Hajhi girl had the makings of a politician. With a twinge of reluctant admiration she acknowledged that Jhezra seemed to have learned from her recent experiences in the Library.

Distracted by her own thoughts Laura didn't catch the queen's response but she was sufficiently alert to notice when the dry voice was directed at her.

'Lisle tells me that you also have been injured, but that there is hope of your recovery,' the queen said and Laura wondered what else Lisle had told her.

'Some hope, your majesty,' she said, keeping her voice cool and clear. 'I wish to be realistic about my chances of a cure but unfortunately I'm finding it difficult to learn what a realistic view *is*. Opinions seem to differ.'

There was a pause and then the queen spoke again, more slowly:

'Then your problem is that there is no such view. The borders of possibility are wider than any single person can imagine. Even a queen.'

'Perhaps the only way to discover what is realistic is to explore every possibility as it comes to you,' Laura said slowly. She didn't want to lose the queen's attention but this kind of jousting with words was more complex than her machinations with the merchant guild in Shattershard.

Already Laura suspected that Lachesis was a clever politician. Her mental image of the queen as Elizabeth I grew stronger and staring into the blur of light and shadow that played across her eyes she tried to make it resolve into shape.

'That would suppose that all possibilities are equally worthy of exploration,' the queen said. 'But I sympathize with your dilemma.' She paused and turning her attention elsewhere asked, 'What is it that ails the young man?'

'The surgeon is attending him now,' Lisle said. 'But the problem may require the knowledge of scholars from another world. I intend to make enquiries while I travel since my duties will shortly take me from you again, with your permission.'

'You have it. Although I will be sorry to lose your counsel again so soon,' the queen said. 'But tonight at least you will stay . . . and your companions also?'

Laura barely listened to Lisle's acceptance and Zoë's and Jhezra's polite murmurs of thanks. Supposedly knowledge of other worlds was kept among Collegiate members but it was blatantly clear that Lisle had told Lachesis about the Doors. It was impossible for Laura to tell through her clouded vision how many other people were in the room but there had been enough moving shapes around the corners of her vision for her to guess that at least some of the queen's court were present.

She was beginning to wonder if every Collegiate member was breaking the rules and the only sin was getting caught.

Morgan stood in the white room and tried to imagine herself as an agent of the Wheel. Staring at the pale haunted face of the stranger in the looking glass she seemed to see two other images overlapping the present.

One was a shy schoolgirl in a second-hand uniform, black hair tangled into dreadlocks and thick make-up shielding her from hostile eyes. The other was a black mage, standing at the gates of the Archon's castle, calling down magic to protect the city she loved.

The reflections disappeared as she imagined a new image of herself as a ruler of worlds, hair streaming like a black flag from the battlements of a castle. Like a witch-queen from one of her favourite fantasies, terrible and beautiful, a dangerous force to be feared or adored. Vespertine had promised her everything: powers, privilege, wealth. The worlds seemed to spin before her like coloured balls and all she had to do was stretch out her hand and take them.

After all, why shouldn't she? Morgan felt a surge of bitterness as she recalled how the Jurists had treated her. Vespertine was right, it was them who'd put her on trial and punished her. If Ciren and Charm hadn't kidnapped her she'd be back on Earth now. Why should she abide by the Collegiate's rules when they'd treated her so unfairly? All Vespertine wanted was for her to use her magic to help him bring peace to the worlds.

Before the servants had taken her back to her room they'd shown her around the villa: the formal precision of the gardens with their raked paths of gravel in between geometric flowerbeds; the elegant simplicity of the chains of connected rooms; and the distant vistas of a world at peace.

That was all she wanted really. Somewhere where she could be happy. She imagined having a place of her own, a palace or castle like Vespertine had promised or just a simple room somewhere that was hers. That was all she wanted, that and Kal by her side. And Vespertine had promised to find him for her.

The twist in her own expression brought her back to herself and she stared into her own eyes with a sense of shock. What would Kal do if the Wheel did find him and bring him to her? What would he think of her for agreeing to work with the people who were taking over his world? She tried to imagine explaining it to him and could only recall the terrible fear that had overcome her when the Jurists challenged her to defend her actions. What if he was disgusted by what she'd become?

Perhaps she could ask Vespertine to find him first, to make Kal a condition of her working for the Wheel. But what then? The vision of herself in the future returned with a vengeance and this time Kal was walking away from her. When they ran away together he'd given her the choice to stay with the Wheel or come with him.

How would he react to being given to her by the Wheel as a reward?

They could do it. Suddenly she had no doubt of that. Vespertine Chalcedony would give the order and Ciren and Charm would set out. They'd find him and kidnap him, as they had kidnapped her. It wouldn't matter what he wanted, they'd say it was for his own good, and they'd bring him back to Chalice and hand him over to Vespertine just as they had handed over Morgan. Because that was what it meant to be an agent of the Wheel.

Morgan felt as if she was coming up for air after having been underwater for a long time. The white walls seemed to close in around her as she realized what Vespertine's promises really meant. He talked about people as if they were things, like prizes to be given or tools to be used. Maybe he *was* right about the way worlds should be run but look at what happened to the people who worked for him.

Back when she'd first met them Ciren and Charm had frightened her with their strangeness but she'd come to think of them as friends. Then in the Library, with Vespertine pulling the strings, they'd been colder and when they'd kidnapped her they'd been different again. Her feelings hadn't mattered to them, nothing mattered except obeying Vespertine's commands, and that was what would happen to her. That was the price she would pay for using her magic to serve him.

Staring into her own eyes, now filled with terrible resolve, Morgan wondered at what point she'd decided to refuse.

After the audience with the queen, Lisle's daughter had taken them to another long wide room where a meal was being served. Zoë thought to herself that in the last few weeks she'd eaten meals on three different worlds and all over the Library and nowadays she never knew what she was going to be offered or when. They'd had breakfasts in the evening and dinner straight after waking up and never the same thing twice in a row.

This time it was skewers of meat dressed with a spicy sauce and a heap of boiled vegetables that tasted like onions and swede. She didn't like it much but she managed to eat most of it after scraping some of the hot sauce off. Jhezra finished her plate as she had everything they'd been offered but Laura toyed with her food, staring off into the middle distance.

'Do you think your eyes are getting better?' Zoë asked her, trying to keep her voice natural, and Laura's eyes tracked slowly in her direction.

'Perhaps . . .' Laura said slowly. 'I can make out colours and shapes a bit. But I'm wondering . . .'

Jhezra looked up from her food, watching Laura with interest.

'Wondering?' she asked.

'Yes . . . I'm wondering if, as Lisle suggests, the improvement is because this world has too little magic for the curse to work . . . then I'll be blind again if we leave here.'

'But you know Lisle wants to go on and leave here through another Door,' Zoë said, worried. 'She thinks that there's a Library faction that can help Kal and . . .'

'Shush . . .' Laura said suddenly and Zoë stopped short.

'We shouldn't talk about that sort of thing here,' Laura said definitely and before Zoë could insist, Jhezra nodded.

'We should go somewhere where we won't be overheard.'

Zoë looked around in surprise. The dining room was almost empty except for a couple of men tending the stone oven built into one wall.

But Jhezra's expression was serious and Zoë held her tongue while they walked together through the palace. It was getting late in the day and when they passed a set of open shutters Zoë could see that it was dark outside. The snow storm had stopped but as she paused to look out she still shivered in the suddenly cold air. The capital city was almost lost under the blanket of heavy whiteness and glimmered almost like the ice palace she had imagined. Up in the sky a large round moon was climbing the sky and behind it another moon, smaller and paler, was coming up from the horizon. The light they shed sparkled from the snow while throwing everything else into shadow so that it was a black and white landscape that Zoë stared down upon.

Jhezra had paused as well and Laura waited for a couple of minutes before asking, 'Why have we stopped?'

'Sorry.' Zoë turned away from the window. If it had only been Jhezra there she would have liked to look longer at the black sky and the white ground. Somehow it had made her feel how large the universe was in a way the library hadn't. But the moment passed and she followed the others up the stairs.

Jhezra led them to a bedroom where some of her and Laura's belongings had been left and as they went in she closed the door behind her.

'What was it that you thought should be said in private?' she said, looking towards Laura.

'I don't think we should speak too freely about Doors and other worlds,' Laura explained and Zoë blinked.

'But Lisle . . .' she began and Laura shook her head suddenly, and started speaking over her.

'Don't you think it's a little odd that Lisle should talk about it at all?' she demanded. 'Come on, Zoë, you ought to know the Collegiate rules by now. World travellers aren't supposed to tell *anyone* about the Doors unless they already know about them.'

'Well, maybe the queen *did* know about them,' Zoë argued and Laura smiled with an air of superiority.

'I'm sure she did, but how could she know unless Lisle had already told her?'

Zoë was going to argue but Jhezra was looking worried.

'Lisle said she could take us across this world and through another Door to a place where there might be a cure for Kal,' Jhezra said. 'Do you believe her, Laura?'

'That depends on her motives,' Laura said, lying back on the bed and staring up at the ceiling. 'She's behaving suspiciously, you have to admit.'

'What do you mean, suspiciously?' Zoë looked from Laura to Jhezra disbelievingly. 'Lisle's been nothing but kind to us: she helped us escape from the Library because she was worried about the Wheel; she's helping Kal when none of the other Jurists would; she's willing to take us to a place where people who actually understand about these things live.'

'Well, you seem to know a lot about it,' Laura said sarcastically and Zoë drew in her breath sharply.

'Do not start another argument,' Jhezra said suddenly and Zoë felt a stab of betrayal. Jhezra seemed to be suddenly supporting Laura and she turned hurt eyes on her and asked, 'Don't you trust Lisle *either*?'

Jhezra leaned back against the door and seemed to be thinking. After a moment she looked back at Zoë and said, 'I do trust Lisle.' Her gaze flickered over to Laura as she added, 'But some of her behaviour is contradictory. In the Library, Lisle was a member of the Jurists who are stern law-givers but here she talks freely in a way we know to be against the rules. Lisle took part in the trial but not everything that happened there was exactly just.'

Zoë couldn't help looking pointedly at Laura at that, but of course she couldn't see her. Jhezra did though and finished abruptly, 'Laura believes Lisle has used her knowledge of other worlds to make Lachesis the queen of this world.'

'What? How?' Zoë stared and Laura shrugged.

'I don't know exactly,' she said. 'But think about it. Lisle said she came from here when she wasn't much older than us. Even just a little time in the Library would have been enough to teach her things about power and politics. If she brought that knowledge back with her she would have used it to help Lachesis overthrow Wutan or whatever his name was.'

'You're just guessing,' Zoe said, uncertainly. 'And even if she did help Lachesis take over why should that mean we can't trust her?'

'I thought you were against people taking over other worlds as a matter of principle?' Laura said and Jhezra frowned at her.

'Laura, Alex was punished for trying to take over Shattershard while you were judged innocent,' the Hajhi girl said with strength in her voice. 'Could Lisle have also made the Jurists or other Collegiate people believe she had done nothing wrong?'

'Or they just don't know about it.' Laura seemed oblivious to the implied criticism. 'This place is utterly in the boondocks. Lisle used an obscure route through the Library and had a secret mark by the right Door. I think the rule is that Collegiate members can do what they like as long as no one can prove it.'

'But that can't be true,' Zoë protested. 'Look, Lisle

was worried about the Wheel. Maybe she's helping us because we're mixed up in that . . . because the Wheel took Morgan away . . . because . . .'

Zoë couldn't go on. Her voice was strained and kept shaking and she realized if she went on any further she'd be in tears. Jhezra seemed to have joined Laura's side and now the suggestion that Lisle couldn't be trusted had hit her hard.

'Zoë?' Jhezra came to sit beside her. 'What's wrong?'

Zoë looked at her friend's dark brown eyes, now serious and concerned, and took a shaky breath.

'It's Morgan,' she said. 'And Alex . . . Those two people from the Wheel . . . they were supposed to be taking them back to Earth. But Morgan was . . . she was terrified of them . . .' She looked towards Laura and couldn't say any more for a moment. Finally, her throat raw, she managed to choke out another few words. 'I know you hate Morgan, Laura . . . but there's Alex too . . . and anyway . . . they're from Earth. We *know* them . . .'

'We should help them,' Jhezra finished for her and then put her arms around Zoë as she cried.

Charm looked down at the figure of her twin, lying crumpled on the grass, and knew that he was right to be afraid. She could feel her lips pulling back into the grimace she called a smile; she could almost hear his thoughts thundering inside his head. So close, a brittle wall of bone was all that separated her from his mind.

She'd always known that he was frightened of her. Known without knowing, without admitting it to herself. It was the reason she'd never breached that frail barrier. She'd told herself they were close enough not to need it, their lives and thoughts entwined as if they were one person not two. And she *had* broken the silent trust. Memories surged like images from a dream and she remembered delving deep into those thoughts, the gates opening, walls crumbling as she strolled through the corridors of Ciren's mind. Then the image of Vespertine Chalcedony came between them like a shadow, erasing the past.

Their patron had done something, changed them somehow. He'd put everything back the way it was and now nothing was the same.

'I did read your mind, but I don't remember it,' Charm said. She bit her lips fiercely, drawing blood, and when that wasn't enough she covered her mouth with her hands and dug her fingers into her face. 'What did I see?'

Ciren didn't answer, he seemed transfixed by fear, his lips moving silently at first and then speaking like someone in a trance.

'Black wheels, spinning. The inside-out tower, white walls closing in, locked Doors, and something hidden . . .'

Struggling to control her own power, Charm realized that Ciren was using his. While she could sense thoughts, he could sense magic and his words made it sound as if magic was alive all around them, seething beneath the surface of the regimented order of Chalice, like the hyacinth vines in the still lake.

Ciren was deep in trance now, not even speaking, his breathing becoming laboured and his eyes glassing over. Not touching him, Charm knelt beside her twin and spoke urgently.

'Ciren, come back.' She tried to will him out of the trance. 'Let go of the magic. Be here. With me.'

The room was silent. Jhezra rubbed Zoë's shoulders as she drew a few shaking breaths. Laura had sat up at the end of the bed and was looking in their direction. It was impossible to tell what she could see or what she was thinking.

'The two of you are not friends,' Jhezra said, hearing her own words fall into the silence. 'But Kal and I were enemies and now I would wish to help him because, as Zoë says, we come from the same world.'

She paused and then spoke again, still thinking it out in her head as she listened to herself:

'Morgan I barely knew but I am sure that she was no more wrong than Alex and I were in fighting for something she thought was right. If what Laura thinks is true then perhaps Lisle has broken the Collegiate rules, but I think we have all agreed by now that Collegiate rules are not always wise or their judges fair.'

She paused. Zoë's breathing had calmed down but her head was bent and Laura's expression was still unreadable. Neither of them spoke.

'The Wheel we know almost nothing about. But we do know they are more knowledgeable than the government of Shattershard, more powerful than the Tetrarchate, more dangerous than the Jurists or any of the Library factions we have met. Those two people were on my world, they know the way to your world, they took Morgan and Alex away with them, and even now they may be preparing to take our worlds over.'

Jhezra realized she had made up her mind.

'I don't want them to take over my people and if I can, I would like to help Alex, and Morgan, escape from them.'

Zoë finally lifted her head and squeezed Jhezra's hand as she sat up. Her face was solemn but determined.

'I want to help Morgan,' she said. 'If it hadn't been for her telling me about the Door under Shattershard we'd be dead by now. I want to help Morgan and . . .'

her mouth twisted in an unhappy smile, ' . . . I want to save Earth from the Wheel.'

'Save Earth?' Laura's voice was suddenly incredulous. 'You think *Earth* is in danger? Look, Zoë, wasn't it you who said that people couldn't just stroll into a military base and walk off with whatever they liked? Just think about it. None of the worlds we've seen are even at industrial revolution level technology. Earth has nuclear warheads! If the Wheel even poke their heads through a Door they won't know what's hit them.'

'The Wheel have magic,' Zoë said, her voice flat.

'Which can't be used on Earth,' Laura said. 'Or Morgan would be the Witch Queen of Weybridge and the rest of us her minions.'

'I understand your doubts, Laura,' Jhezra said, keeping her arm around Zoë's shoulders comfortingly. 'But the Wheel are cunning. Those two people convinced the Jurists they could be trusted. And if they can take over your world in some way, those weapons you speak of will belong to them, to aid them in taking over new worlds.'

Jhezra and Zoë both looked at Laura and for a moment her green gaze cleared as if she could see them.

'Yes,' she said slowly. 'That's a thought. If you had really strong magic and nuclear age weapons you probably could go out and conquer the universe.'

# 8

It wasn't exactly an awesome feat of bravery, Alex told himself. Asking to speak to the barrack commander wasn't about to qualify him for the order of merit, and even if it didn't work it probably wouldn't go horribly wrong. At least that's what he tried to hold in his mind as he was shown up to the man's office.

It had been a long day of training and exercises which was doubtless why his legs felt shaky as he crossed the room and stood before the commander's desk. The rest of the room was bare, even the surface of the desk hardly had any paper on it, aside from a notebook that Alex recognized as his own.

The commander flipped through the first couple of pages, the only ones to have been filled in, before fixing Alex with a stern look.

'You asked to see me, soldier,' he said.

'Yes, sir,' Alex replied, staring straight in front of him and trying to keep to a military bearing.

'Well, what is it that you want?' the commander barked. 'Finding the training too tough, are you?'

'No, sir.' Alex shook his head and the commander frowned, glancing back at the papers on the desk.

'Says here the armsmaster passed you as a fair swordsman, you write a neat script, and apparently you have a head on your shoulders. Perhaps you think you already know all there is to learn?'

'No, sir,' Alex repeated, relaxing very slightly. So far this encounter was going the way he'd expected.

The commander flipped the pieces of paper about some more but he seemed to have run out of interest in them and finally he ordered, 'Well, my time's valuable and you're taking up too much of it. Say your piece and make it brief.'

This was where it all got tricky and Alex reminded himself that this man would expect him to be a bit wary, he didn't have to keep up a pretence of complete calm, just be convincing.

'It's about this assignment I've been given by my Salvage instructor,' he said. 'I don't see how to complete the work.'

Here the commander did look back down at Alex's notebook.

'Assignment seems clear to me,' he said. 'Describe your originating world and note where appropriate the location of its Doors. What's the problem there?'

'I don't think the instructor will understand my answers,' Alex said coolly. As the commander's face began to get red he added for good measure, 'Or that anyone else here will, either.'

'You think we're stupid?' The commander seemed more incredulous than outraged; possibly he simply couldn't believe what Alex was saying.

'No, sir,' Alex replied, trying not to push it too far.

'It's simply that my home world seems more technologically advanced than Chalice, or any other world of the Collegiate that I've seen so far. My description wouldn't make any sense to someone who hadn't heard of electricity or the industrial revolution or nuclear power.'

'You can't explain these things yourself?' the commander asked suspiciously and Alex shook his head again.

'No, sir,' he said. 'Certainly not in the time available for the assignment. It would take months, if not years, to write down everything I know about my world. I may not be a very good student here, sir, but on Earth I was in the top stream of my school in science. I might have gone for Oxford or Cambridge if I'd stayed.'

The commander said nothing for a moment and Alex had to resist the temptation to cross his fingers. He didn't know how many of his words would translate and was counting on the fact that not all of them would. But now he had to be very careful.

'Permission to speak freely, sir?' he asked and the commander nodded sharply.

'Very well.'

'I'm not sure why I was assigned to be Salvaged here, sir. I've had some experience with fighting but really I'm more on the technical side. If the Wheel have any people working on warfare, siege weapons, and the sort of military advancement that doesn't involve magic, I might be better able to explain myself to them. But the agents who brought me in seemed more concerned with the girl I was travelling with, so I didn't have an opportunity before now to discuss how I might serve the Wheel. Sir.'

He stopped speaking and straightened a bit more, trying to adopt the pose of a bandbox soldier. The commander hadn't said anything and he had a frown plastered across his face but it was thoughtful rather than angry. Alex concentrated on not showing his relief. He had been right! The sinister twins had just dumped him here; they were obviously more important than this commander and hadn't bothered to make a report about the circumstances of his and Morgan's capture.

Alex tried not to let his own face show anything other than respectful obedience. He hadn't asked to be taken out of Salvage, just shown the understandable frustration of a specialist shunted into the wrong job. If he had been a magician like Morgan he'd probably have been sent off for whatever they were putting her through right now. All he was really asking was to be put to work with whatever the Wheel had that passed for a scientific R and D team.

'This fighting you've done,' the commander said. 'Where was that, exactly?'

'I never discovered the name of the world, sir. But the ruling government were called the Tetrarchate. I was employed as a military adviser by a clan of nomads trying to take control of a fortified city. My team sabotaged the mechanism controlling the main gate while other troops used explosive weapons of my design to attack the city militia and two divisions of the Tetrarchate army.'

'And were you successful?'

'Not ultimately,' Alex said slowly. 'We did sabotage the gates but the battle was ended abruptly when the mages stepped in.'

For the first time he was grateful for the trial the Jurists had put him through. He'd messed that up, not taking it seriously enough, while Morgan had made a worse hash of it still. But he'd seen how Laura's twisting the facts, Jhezra's tribal honour, and Zoë's outright honesty had worked for them.

'Very well, soldier,' the commander said, coming to a decision. 'I've heard what you've said and I'll take your request to be transferred to a different Salvaging group under advisement. In the meantime I'll excuse you from basic orientation so that you can write a detailed report on your role as military adviser to these nomads.'

'Yes, sir.' Alex saluted.

'Dismissed.'

Leaving the commander's office with a confident stride, Alex hoped his gamble would pay off. But almost immediately that thought was followed by how to write up the Shattershard conflict in a way that made him look good. Jhezra had considered the whole affair a disaster, for the tribes as well as the city people, but Jhezra wasn't the one trapped in a training camp for world conquerors. As he walked back to his barracks he wondered where she was and what she was doing now.

Jhezra was walking softly through the Winter Palace, her footsteps muffled by the thick soft furs on the stone floor. She kept to the darker sides of the rooms but she didn't try to hide, instead she moved slowly, looking at the few pieces of furniture as if studying the decoration.

When Jhezra had parted from the others very little had been decided. Zoë had gone back to her room, looking tired and drained, once Laura had agreed that they would discuss the situation with Lisle tomorrow. After she'd left Jhezra had said she was going for a walk. Laura hadn't even looked in her direction but she had nodded as if she had guessed what Jhezra was planning to do.

It wasn't spying, not exactly. No one had told her she wasn't allowed to explore the palace. But it was night and the halls were mostly empty and Jhezra kept away from the places of light and activity. Instead she retraced the route to the room where the queen had received them. It was a smaller room partitioned off from one of the long halls and Jhezra had expected there to be guards at the door. They were there, and when she saw them in the distance she drifted idly away and back to the staircase where a window had been open. It was closed now but she found it easy to lift the bar aside and unbolt the shutters. Then she glanced briefly down the corridor and stepped on to the windowsill.

It was as she had spotted earlier: a wooden walkway ran around this side of the building. It was slippery with frozen water and Jhezra stepped out carefully, leaving the shutters open behind her. She shivered in the cold air before edging closer to the walls as she walked quietly along the outside of the palace. Forty steps along and she was past the hall where the guards had been, another twenty brought her up to a shuttered window and she stood still outside it listening.

There were voices inside and in the still crisp air they carried softly to Jhezra's ears. The woman speaking was Lisle.

' . . . always been a problem,' she was saying. 'The marcher barons were a thorn in Wutan's side as well.'

'For once I sympathize with my predecessor,' Queen Lachesis's voice replied drily. 'I imagine his method of dealing with them was more direct.'

'Perhaps that wouldn't hurt,' Lisle suggested. 'Make an example of a few and the others will respect you more.'

'And give the vacillators more reason to think me tyrannical,' the queen returned.

'You must do as you think wise.' Lisle's voice was noncommittal but the queen laughed.

'With so much wisdom at my command, my problem is distinguishing which counsel is best,' she said. 'I must be "realistic", as your young companion wishes to be.'

'That one has the makings of a politician who could rival any counsel I can give you,' Lisle told her. 'Laura had the measure of the Jurists in under a day.'

'So did my Spymaster,' Lachesis said. 'Caravaggion stayed a few days here after bringing your messages. He seemed to think they would crumble soon.'

'Not long now, I think,' Lisle agreed. 'They're already snowblind enough to stone a dog and feed a wolf.'

'So you will travel to warn Caravaggion?' Lachesis asked. 'Will his world fight if it comes to it?'

'Not overtly,' Lisle said. 'It's not their way. But they will have some plan, I'm sure of it.'

'And these children you plan to take with you?'

'May be useful,' Lisle said. 'In fact I have a suspicion that one of them . . .'

Her voice lowered and Jhezra crouched to hear better. The sudden change of posture made her foot slide and she tried to stop herself by grabbing at the windowsill. Icicles snapped from the edge of the ledge and her elbow knocked painfully against the wall as she fell to her knees on the walkway.

The sound of voices was quelled and then suddenly increased and she heard the sound of footsteps hurrying towards the window.

The twins rode slowly back to the villa, Charm leading Ciren's horse as he sat slumped over the pommel of his saddle. The use of his magic had left him feeling drained and Charm had barely spoken as she'd helped him back to his feet, aside to say that they should go back.

Of course they had to go back, Ciren knew that.

Where else would they go? And yet as the elegant lines of the villa rose up before them Ciren felt a deepening sense of pressure, a headache settling in at the back of his skull and weariness like a grey umbrella overshadowing him from above.

'We need to talk,' he said, dragging the words up from inside himself.

It took Charm so long to respond that he wasn't sure if he had spoken out loud.

'Perhaps you should rest?' she suggested diffidently, as they rode in at the stable entrance.

Her eyes didn't meet his and he felt dizzy again as he swung down from the horse. The ground beneath his feet felt unstable and he tried again to find words.

'Will you tell Vespertine . . . ?'

'What's to tell?' Charm spoke quickly. Throwing the reins of both horses to the servants, she turned to extend him her arm. 'Shall I help you upstairs?'

'I'm all right,' Ciren told her and she dropped her hand quickly, still not looking at him directly.

As they went inside they walked together in silence, and Ciren tried to think past the throbbing in his head. He would have liked to accept Charm's support but he didn't know what it entailed. His memory was still snarled on a tangle of half-glimpsed images and what he felt was simple and natural one moment was distorted and obscene the next.

Charm pushed open the door of their shared rooms, stepping back to enter behind him and he felt his own start of surprise echoed a moment later as they realized they were not alone. Morgan was waiting for them; standing at a window and looking down at the sheltered garden at the centre of the villa.

'What are you doing here?' Charm asked and Morgan raised her head to look at them, the bleakness of her expression replaced with distance, as if she stared at them from unimaginably far away.

'I never invited the two of you to my room either, back in Shattershard,' she said. 'But you came anyway.'

Ciren felt her words sear in him like brands and he reached for the back of a chair to support himself.

'What do you want?' he asked.

Morgan's mouth stretched into a grisly smile and he flinched back from it, afraid for a moment that she had acquired Charm's power.

'I want to know who you are,' she said.

Zoë hadn't gone back to her room. Instead she had gone to check on Kal. The surgeon was in the small bedroom when she got there and she watched as he carefully lifted each of Kal's eyelids to peer into his eyes and took his pulse. He was a middle-aged man and instead of the leather and fur she'd seen everyone else wearing he wore a brown shirt and trousers under a long cloak made of wool.

Sitting back from the bed he nodded at Zoë, and beckoned her into the room, gesturing at a chair at Kal's bedside.

'Have you come to sit with your friend?' he asked. 'That's well for him. It might be that he can tell you are here.'

'Do you really think so?' Zoë asked doubtfully.

'Perhaps.' The surgeon looked at Kal's still body thoughtfully and then said, 'There is something I would like to try but I don't know your customs.'

'*My* customs?' Zoë was confused and the surgeon pointed at Kal's head, to where the silvery mesh of his Archon's crown circled his forehead.

'I would like to remove this sigil of rank from his

brow,' the man explained slowly. 'I think perhaps it has poisoned the blood, wherefore he sleeps.'

'Blood poisoning?' Zoë shook her head. 'That can't be right, it's not that sort of problem.'

'But yes, look.' The surgeon stood up and leaned forward over the bed to point more definitively at where the spiky metal of the crown was tangled up in Kal's golden hair.

Zoë leaned forward as well to peer at where he was pointing and tried to understand what he could possibly mean.

'I don't see any blood,' she said. 'But those spikes do look awfully sharp.'

'The points of the metal are very thin,' the surgeon said. 'And where they touch the skin it is puckered very slightly as if the points have penetrated there. Now, see what happens when I touch it . . .'

Zoë held still as the surgeon took a smoothed piece of wood like a miniature ruler and parted some strands of Kal's hair before trying to lift away a strand of the metal mesh. Zoë saw a spark arc across the crown and the surgeon pulled back quickly before it reached his hand. But now there was blood, a tiny bead of it on Kal's forehead, where previously the crown had touched it.

'You see?' the surgeon said and she looked at him with wide eyes. 'I think it should be removed,' he went on. 'But there may be some danger.' He looked at her questioningly. 'What do you think?'

Zoë looked down at the sleeping boy. There was no one here who had the right to make that kind of decision for him. What if removing the crown made him worse in some way or even killed him? If she knew anything about him other than what Jhezra or Laura had mentioned she might have some idea about what he would have wanted.

The surgeon was still waiting and she wondered if he was really skilled enough to deduce something that none of the magicians in the Library had noticed. But his manner was so thoughtful and considered that somehow it was more convincing than if he had tried to persuade her that he knew what he was doing. Laura's blindness had been partly cured by visiting this world where magic was scarce, perhaps this was the only place where Kal could be cured of the spell on him as well.

'I think you should try taking it off,' she said.

'Very well.' The surgeon reached for his box of implements lying at his side and Zoë felt sick with nerves.

'You're going to do it now?' she asked.

'His heartbeat is laboured and his skin is flushed; the cold of winter is not good for sleeping sickness,' the surgeon told her, as he looked through the box and took out a polished wooden set of tongs. 'If there is no taboo broken by it, the sigil should be removed as soon as possible.' He looked across at Zoë and said, 'You don't have to watch.'

She didn't say anything but she didn't move either and the surgeon took a pair of thin white leather gloves from the box and put them on. Taking up the tongs and the short wooden ruler again he leaned over Kal and his face set in concentration.

A spark sizzled; two more flashed across the mesh circlet. Zoë tucked her legs under the chair and clung on to the seat with her hands, trying to see past the surgeon's careful probing fingers. Then, suddenly, there was a crackling and a scatter of bright spots of light across Zoë's vision, and the surgeon had pulled back with the Archon's crown in his hands. Kal's body jerked once convulsively and then fell back on the bed and Zoë could see more blood beading in his hair.

The surgeon put the crown aside with clumsy haste

and stripped off his gloves after it. They were singed with black marks and beneath them his long white hands were covered in the bumps of blisters.

'What happened?' Zoë asked, looking frantically between him and Kal, and the surgeon bent over Kal's body, listening to his chest.

'He breathes, his heart beats,' the man said and moved back. 'I think it was for the best. Will you watch him while I clean my hands? If there is poison I must not be infected by it.'

'OK,' Zoë said uncertainly and the surgeon looked consideringly at her for a moment.

'I won't be far,' he assured her. 'A shout will bring me if anything changes.'

She nodded and with that he left the room.

Moving closer to the bed Zoë stared down at Kal's face, knotted in a frown. A trickle of blood was sliding down his forehead and Zoë used the corner of a blanket to wipe it away before it could drop into his eyes. The crown was off but there was still no sign of him waking and she checked his pulse again anxiously. His skin was cold under her hand and her fingers tingled as if he was still in the static field, making it hard to tell if his heart-beat was fast or slow.

Her eyes shifted to the crown, lying on the chest of drawers, and she shuddered convulsively at the spiked mesh. She couldn't believe it was blood poisoning that had affected Kal but she didn't like the thought of thorns too thin to see digging into flesh. Kal was thin, his face almost waxen, and there were blue-grey shadows in the corners of his eyes. She wondered if they could really have taken the crown off at any time and if he would now recover. *This is how the prince must have felt about Snow White,* she thought. *The poisoned apple fell out of her mouth and while he was wondering what it meant . . .*

But Kal still showed no sign of waking. Zoë wiped away another bead of blood, leaning closer as she did so. Slowly she bent her head until she felt Kal's faint breath against her face. His skin was cold but his mouth was warm when she kissed him.

Morgan didn't know what she'd expected. But what she got was no response at all. The twins simply stared at her, apparently frozen in place by her question.

'I already know you're ciphers,' she said. 'That you do whatever Vespertine tells you. What I want to know is why you do it? Is it money, or power, or just because you fancy yourselves dressed in black? He's already promised me the world . . . what did he promise you?'

The twins looked shell-shocked and Morgan felt a part of her relish the contrast. When they'd brought her to this place, she'd been the one in shock, now they were slumped like puppets with cut strings.

'You knew what you were doing when you brought me here,' she said. 'You handed me over to Vespertine to be brainwashed and you probably know what the punishment is for saying no. You used to be people once, maybe strange and unusual ones, but you had feelings. Now, it's like you're dead inside.' She shook her head. 'What kind of person does that? Hands someone over to something they hate? Vespertine tried to persuade me to do it and I almost believed him. But then I realized that was what you did to me.'

The words were pouring out of her now in a torrent and Morgan realized this was something she'd wanted to say for a long time. She'd blamed herself for what had happened, but now she'd found a different target for her anger and disappointment. Perhaps she wasn't so pathetic after all, or her magic as deadly. Finally she was finding the words she wished she could have spoken to the Jurists.

'You've been lying to me ever since I first met you,' she said, looking first at Ciren. 'You lied about the Collegiate and you tried to hide what the Wheel were doing on Kal's world.' Her gaze shifted to Charm and she went on. 'You lied when you promised not to read my mind and you lied when you pretended you could read Kal.'

As she spoke Morgan realized that in the end she was as much confused as betrayed.

'Why do you do it?' she asked the twins. 'Laura lies because she's a power-hungry bitch who'd step on anyone who got in her way. But you two, I don't think you even know why you do it. It's like you've sold your souls and now there's nothing even human about you any more.'

Stepping away from the window, she took a step towards them and was surprised when they both flinched. She felt the magic inside her uncoil at this sudden recognition of her power, filling her with energy.

'Anyway,' she concluded. 'I just wanted you to know that I'm not going to join the Wheel, whatever Vespertine says. Because I'd rather die than be like you.'

She had to leave then, turning her back on the horror with which the twins were staring at her, as if she'd spoken the words of their most feared nightmare. But when her hand was on the door, she stopped. It was Kal she was doing this for, she reminded herself, and Kal wouldn't want her to do this, to destroy someone so completely.

'I'm sorry,' she said, swallowing, forcing her magic and her anger back down. She didn't turn to meet those black-violet eyes, speaking instead to the wall. 'I don't know what he did to you to make you like this. But whatever it is . . . it's not worth it.'

It seemed to Kal as if he was falling upwards, the visions of tortured metal and molten rock sinking down below him as he floated free and suddenly light. If that had been real, perhaps he was dreaming now. He lay on something as soft as velvet, silky hair fell forward into his face from someone leaning over him, and he reached up for the kiss he could still feel on his lips.

'Morgan . . .' he said and woke.

# 9

Zoë jumped back as if she had been scalded, half falling into the chair behind her. Kal pulled himself upright, grey eyes wide with confusion as he stared at her, and the door opened with a sudden crack. She turned to catch a glimpse of the surgeon before a fur-clad soldier stepped past him and looked at Zoë with a grim expression.

'You will come with me,' she said.

Zoë stumbled and the guard put a hand on her arm before hustling her out of the room. The surgeon's eyes met hers with a puzzled look before he slipped past her into the room and Zoë was firmly escorted away.

Trying to collect her thoughts Zoë wasn't sure what was happening as the soldier hurried her down one staircase, then another, then one more. It wasn't until she was being nudged down a fourth that Zoë found words to protest.

'What's going on?' she asked and the woman sneered at her.

'We don't much like spies here,' she said. 'Now go on with you.'

'Spies? What—' but she didn't have time to ask any more. She had taken five steps down the staircase and the soldier was moving back up to take hold of a wooden shutter on the floor. In one smooth movement she lifted it and then let it fall like a lid over the top of the staircase, shutting Zoë on the other side and in the dark.

'Hey!' she shouted and jumped to try and push the trapdoor up but it seemed to be stuck, even when she heaved with all her strength. 'Come back!' she shouted through the door but nobody replied. 'This isn't fair . . .'

Finally she gave up and sat forlornly on the stairway, burying her head in her hands.

Ciren raised his head to look at Charm and met the same terrible knowledge in her eyes that he knew was reflected in his own.

'What did he do to us?' he asked. 'Do you know?'

'I don't know,' she said softly. 'I saw something . . . in your mind . . . but it was hidden.' She took a step back from him while the memory of that overcame him. 'Forgive me,' she said. 'I don't know anything.'

'We have to know,' Ciren said. He slammed his hand down on the table so hard it hurt but he clung to the pain, concentrating on it as something real in contrast to the swirling images in his head. 'Before he does it again, floods our minds clean again so that we don't even remember our doubts. We need to know the secrets we're hiding from ourselves.'

'For Morgan's sake?' Charm asked. 'Because she's facing him alone?'

'For our sake,' Ciren told her. 'Yours and mine. So that we don't have to be this thing we are, this thing that isn't human, that she would rather die than become.'

'Then . . .' Charm hesitated. 'Do you want me to do it again . . . to read your . . .'

'No!' Ciren cut her off abruptly. 'There's another way,' he said. 'Vespertine has books, records. Perhaps they hold the key to our past.'

Charm considered that for a moment, then slowly she nodded.

'I looked for our history once,' she said. 'Back in the Great Library. But the Wheel only had one book that mentioned us.'

'What did it say?' Ciren asked, his voice hushed, and Charm lifted her shoulders with a gesture of futility.

'Nothing helpful,' she said. 'It said Vespertine had announced a new asset. Juvenile mages acquired through sources on his home world. Then that we would be initiated into the Wheel.'

'I don't understand,' Ciren said flatly. 'That makes no sense. We didn't come from this world.' The feelings of sick dizziness returned as he said the words and he swallowed, trying to force it back. 'It sounds as if someone sold us to him. But I don't remember anything like that.'

'Neither do I,' his twin replied and they stood in silence for a moment, stalled by their inability to remember their past. 'What if Vespertine doesn't keep records?' Charm asked finally. 'What if he's the only one who knows the truth?'

Ciren shivered. It seemed to him that Charm had always accepted their patron's rule over them more easily than he had. Even now, although he could tell she was worried by the thought of approaching Vespertine, it didn't engender in her the same creeping dread that it did for him.

'There are records we know he keeps,' he said,

wetting his lips. 'Our journals; we've been writing them for as long as I can remember, and giving them to him.' It suddenly seemed obscene that Vespertine had access to their secret thoughts when they couldn't even call their souls their own. Stiffening his shoulders he said, 'That's what we have to look for. He keeps them in his study. In the inner sanctum.'

'Then that's where we must go,' Charm replied.

Before they left the room Charm picked up her sword belt and buckled it around her waist. Her eyes met his silently and Ciren reached for his bow. It occurred to him that the meaning of having a home was that if you knew you might be leaving for ever you would turn back for a last look at what you were leaving behind.

As they left the room together neither of them looked back.

Kal had been brought up to believe that a prince should never swear or shout or throw things at those who served him. Even as a small child he'd known that tantrums were not permitted; fits of temper were inappropriate for someone who was supposed to be a leader of men. For the first time he broke all those rules at once.

He tore himself out of bed, demanding to know what had happened to Morgan, pushing past the ineffectual attempts to restrain him until more guards were called and he was carried back, raging all the while and fighting with what little strength remained to him. The guards finally shut him into the strange bedchamber and he'd cursed them fully and freely from behind the closed door, tearing the room apart in an effort to find something that would batter it down, before finally giving in to his emotions and weeping like a child.

Something sliced into his hands, as sharp as the edge of a sword, and he looked down to see that he was holding a barbed net. It was a moment before he recognized it as the Archon's crown, inexplicably no longer in its accustomed position on his head. Reflexively he reached to put it there and paused, motion arrested instead.

The gods only knew how much time had passed since he stood in the Convening Court of the Jurists and pleaded Morgan's cause, but he knew that it must have done because of the images that had haunted his dreams. In all those dreams the crown had been there, caging him within its net of silver and gold. Now the force of that memory overcame him and his anger melted away as he slumped back on the bed, staring at the thing now lying innocently in his hands.

'I remember . . .' he whispered, in the sudden silence of the room.

He had protested when the Jurists turned Morgan over to the twins and as he reached for his sword, Dalandran the Jurist mage had cast a spell, which rippled across the air and reached out for him. But before whatever it was could touch him the crown had tightened, and a ice-water feeling had rushed through his body.

But now that memory seemed years distant, separated by the visions of his dreams. He had seen his father, racked by the sickness that had killed him, lying in state during his last days. And then it had been him lying in that bed, the Archon's crown a tight band about his head, the cold spikes piercing his brain and the fever knotting his body. He had died then, the first of many deaths. A warrior death-struck on the battlefield, a small child falling from a great height, a woman beaten and bruised and in pain. Every death had been different except for the eternal constant, the freezing, burning points of the Archon's crown.

There'd been nowhere to hide, no way of escaping the flood of images, and the nightmare had swept him further and further back through time, through the lives of his ancestors. The Archons of Shattershard, people whose histories he'd read, became horribly real in those flashes of their death moments as they struggled and fought for each last breath.

And then had come the worst death of all: a nightmare of screaming silver and burning gold, metal tearing like paper and rocks melting into liquid, and a terrible fall that seemed to last for ever, as stars of pain blossomed in the black void of his head. He had died again then, eyelids burned away and eyes open to a terrible scorching sky as he lay in a crater of boiling blackened rock, the shattered shards of a mountain.

Kal looked down at his hands, wet with blood, holding the spiked circlet of the crown. It had been trying to protect him, he knew that with the same certainty that he knew his own name, and he wondered how that could be when the dreams it had brought had all been nightmares.

Alex had been busily writing in his book, expanding the ideas he'd expressed to the commander, when Reck arrived in the dormitory room.

'New orders,' the young man had snapped. 'You're to go to the villa immediately.' He hesitated before adding, 'I don't know what you've done to annoy him but the commander wants you sent to the Founder for further questioning.' There was a flicker of something in Reck's eyes and Alex realized with some surprise that the squad leader was actually sorry for him.

'Thank you, sir,' he said politely and Reck sneered deliberately.

'Good luck, Salvager,' he said in what sounded like an insult but Alex thought might actually be genuinely meant. He didn't have any way to answer. Instead, he headed out of the barracks and down the road he was told would take him to the villa.

If he hadn't been told this world was the centre of operations for the Wheel, he wouldn't have guessed it. Apart from the grey tinge of the sky and the roads paved with stone instead of tarmac, he might have been back on Earth. There was nothing like a wizard's castle or fortress but he realized that this at least showed the power of the Wheel. They were certain enough of their other defences that no one here was expected to be a threat.

His plan had got him this far, out of the barracks at least. But he'd been hoping he might have been transferred off this world, away from the zombie-like presence of the twins, or their mysterious master. Of course, being sent to the villa meant he'd been taken seriously, and there'd always been the chance the barrack commander would laugh at his claims to special knowledge. But now he would have to prove that he was telling the truth.

His footsteps slowed as he approached the plain stone building of the villa. It seemed likely that he was going to be questioned by someone closer to the centre of power than the barrack commander and he wondered how long it would be possible to spin out his knowledge. He'd written as obscurely as he dared in his book, only hinting at the technological skills of Earth. But sooner or later someone was going to ask him how to construct a nuclear power plant or an intercontinental ballistic missile and then the shit would really hit the fan.

Alex wasn't even sure if he could make such a thing but he had a horrible certainty that, if the leaders of the

Wheel did believe him, they'd start building uranium mines across every planet they controlled. Alex had once had fantasies of leading the tribes like Lawrence of Arabia, but now it seemed more likely he would end up in the centre of a Hiroshima disaster.

Coming to a standstill on the smooth roadway, Alex wondered if he had the nerve to go through with this. Every impulse in his body was suggesting that he should run, leave this road, find a hiding place, maybe try to sneak back through the Door at night. It was stupid, he told himself. He wouldn't have a chance and he'd lose whatever credibility he'd managed to build up so far. But right now anything seemed like a better option than confronting whatever was waiting in the grey humped shape of the villa.

He felt the comforting weight of the sword at his hip and told himself the Wheel were civilized, they'd believe him when he explained what science could accomplish. Perhaps they'd put him in charge of a project and he'd have time to consider his options. Perhaps working for the Wheel wouldn't be all that bad. Or maybe they'd let him back into the Library and he'd find another faction to defect to.

*There are always options,* he told himself, his feet starting to move again and carrying him on down the road. *You just have to find them.* But even though he kept walking he couldn't escape the feeling that he was coming to the end of the line.

The guards who had come for Laura had been more polite than she expected. Even when they were forcing her at sword-point through the halls of the winter palace, rough hands that had seized hold of her had only been to prevent her from falling. When they had finally abandoned her in a room so dark she couldn't even see a blurred light, she'd already given up any attempt to reason with them.

Conversely, Zoë had argued to the very end. Laura had heard her coming from the room above, begging for an explanation. Obviously annoyed, the guards had shoved her down the staircase, possibly not wanting to give Laura the opportunity to escape. As the sound of the trapdoor shutting boomed through the room Laura heard Zoë finally give up.

'This isn't fair . . .' she said, bitterly.

'Since when was life fair?' Laura asked.

There was a rustle of sound as Zoë jerked into awareness that she was not alone. When her voice came again it was heavy with suspicion.

'Laura?' she asked and Laura laughed.

'If you're thinking this is all my fault, you can forget it,' she said. 'This time it's your friend Jhezra who's landed us in this mess.'

'If that's true, you probably egged her into whatever it was,' Zoë snapped back.

'I didn't have to,' Laura said. 'While you were mooning about over Kal, Jhezra was actually thinking for a change. You might believe whatever Lisle tells you but Jhezra wanted to find out what she's saying to other people. Since we're now under house arrest, I expect she was caught.'

'Then you better hope I was right about Lisle being a good person,' Zoë said sharply. 'Because if I'm wrong we're in deep trouble now.'

Laura said nothing for a moment, realizing the truth of that. Zoë might be naive but every now and again she'd say something that gave Laura pause for thought. However, it was irritating the way she could seem so oblivious to what Laura found so clear.

'Sometimes I think you're the one who's blind,' she said out loud. 'Here we are in a dark dank cell and you're still finding excuses for Lisle. How can you still be that trusting?'

'I'm not!' Zoë said hotly. Then after a moment she spoke again, her words slow and careful. 'What if everyone were like you, Laura, cold and calculating . . . then you'd never find anyone to believe your lies.'

'Oh, for God's sake.' Laura was surprised at her own anger but she couldn't seem to stop herself. 'What is it with you and this schoolgirl goody-goody ethic. Why can't you accept that the rules have changed? That there's no one you can really trust and no one looking out for you except yourself?'

'Because that's not true,' Zoë said immediately. 'I trust Jhezra and Lisle because they've never given me any reason not to. And even you, you trust people. You trust me and Jhezra to go on looking after you and telling you things even when you treat us like your servants.'

Zoë's voice gained strength as she concluded, 'You know, Laura, you think you're so clever not to trust people. You don't even try to fit in, to convince people to like you, because you're too busy thinking of ways to use them. Don't you even care that there's no one who likes or trusts you? Or if they do it's because you lied to them?'

The determination that had carried Morgan to the twins' rooms had crumbled as she left them. All this time she'd been feeling like a victim, betrayed and led astray by people she'd trusted. But what she had seen in their haunted eyes as she told them what she thought of them had reversed everything and her righteous fury had been followed by shame.

In the grey villa she'd almost forgotten her own magic, burying it and everything else deep inside her so that she wouldn't have to think or feel. Now she could sense it rising up inside her like a fountain, her heart fluttering and her hands shaking as she fought to control it. The Jurists had been right when they'd called her a rogue mage and it scared her to realize how little control she had over her own power.

She could have used her magic on the twins, she was sure of it; she'd been close to it as she'd finally let out her rage. But in that moment of shame that had succeeded it she had seen them through someone else's eyes, remembering the twins as they had been when she'd thought they were her friends. It was Vespertine who'd turned them into vicious killers, and they were like abused children, too frightened of him to admit their own terror.

Morgan would have liked to stay angry with them, but it wasn't anger she felt now, it was fear. Vespertine had spoken kindly to her, had seemed gentle and caring, like a grandfather or an uncle. It was frightening to realize that must have all been an act. How would he respond when she told him she wouldn't do what he wanted? All she knew about the ancient patron of the Wheel was that he was powerful enough to control the twins like puppets, and so far she'd only seen a fraction of that power.

She hadn't been thinking clearly since she got to this place and with that realization came the solution. She wouldn't wait for Vespertine to discover and punish her disobedience. She'd simply leave. Maybe it wouldn't get her very far, since the only Door she knew of was guarded and beyond that lay miles and miles of Library all under the control of the Wheel. But it had to be a better idea than walking straight into the lion's den.

As she changed direction, looking instead for a way

out, she remembered that uncoiling of magic inside her. She hadn't tried to use her magic to do so much as light a candle since blinding Laura but now she searched inside herself for the power she'd been told was there. She wasn't intending to try to be a hero, all she wanted was to get out, but if someone came for her she'd use whatever weapons she had. This time she wouldn't surrender without a fight.

When the Wolves had come for her Jhezra had more sense than to try to run. Caught as she was on a slippery walkway on the second floor of the palace, she knew she wouldn't get far. Besides, she couldn't abandon Zoë and Laura. Instead she let herself be pulled in through the opened window and searched for weapons.

She hadn't worn the scimitar but they took her sickle dagger and the smaller eating knife she carried. Meanwhile the queen and Lisle had watched from a safe distance, surrounded by more of the guards. When Lisle's daughter arrived the Wolves had fallen back, only two of them holding Jhezra in place.

'Your majesty, mother, are you all right?' Siffany asked first and the queen nodded sharply.

'Yes, yes,' she said. 'The Wolves came in the moment we noticed the disturbance. This one,' her gaze pierced Jhezra, 'was spying outside on the walkway.'

'Why?' Lisle interrupted and then bowed in apology. 'Forgive me, majesty, but I'm surprised. This isn't like Jhezra.'

'You are wrong,' Jhezra said firmly. 'Many of my people are spies, we've had to be, our oppressors gave us no choice. And we do not sit idly while matters affecting our future are decided in secret by those who call themselves our rulers.' She met the queen's stare with a level gaze.

Siffany looked appalled and the Wolves' expressions were grim, but Lisle threw back her head and laughed.

'You see what I mean,' she said, turning to the queen with a smile. 'Jhezra doesn't have it in her to do a dishonourable thing. I can well see why she'd have cause to be suspicious of me.'

The queen nodded slowly. 'Yes,' she said. 'I remember a time when I too was excluded from the secret counsels of the wise.' Her expression was bitter as she looked into space, and no one spoke to disturb her thoughts. 'But you need not fear,' she said at last, returning to the here and now and looking at Jhezra. 'No one need fear to speak with honesty while Lachesis sits on the Wolfshead throne.'

At her words the Wolves released Jhezra and, after a sharp signal from Siffany, her dagger and knife were returned.

'Zoë and Laura, and the Archon Kal,' Lisle said suddenly and her eyes narrowed as she looked across at her daughter. 'If there was an alarm they will be suspect . . .'

'I'll see to it,' Siffany said quickly at a look from the queen.

'Bring them here.' Lachesis spoke just as Jhezra was about to protest again. 'The Wolves will certainly have acted to secure them but you will see yourself that they will not have been harmed.'

She spoke with utter confidence and Jhezra hoped that she was right. There was a grimness in Siffany's expression as she and the rest of the guards left the room that suggested she was worried the Wolves might have been over-zealous in their work.

Charm and Ciren weren't challenged by the grey-robed servitors as they made their way through the villa to the study at its centre. It was late afternoon, late enough that Vespertine would probably be resting. But as they reached the curtain that concealed the hidden door, Charm turned to look at her twin.

'Is he inside?' she asked. 'Can you sense his magic?'

Ciren looked sick as he leaned against the grey-shrouded wall and extended his senses, but this time he was able to pull back out of the trance after only a few seconds.

'Magic is foggy in there,' he said uncertainly. 'There are spells all around us, in the tapestries . . . But I don't think he's in there.'

'We should be swift, all the same,' Charm said, and opened the door.

The room was empty. The grey fabric that clung to the walls, ceiling, and floor was all that awaited them but both twins were tense, avoiding the touch of the wall coverings as if it were hanks of cobweb rather than expensive cloth. There was no furniture aside from Vespertine's chair but as they looked uneasily around the room, Ciren pointed to the walls.

'Shelves behind that?' he suggested softly. 'Like in the Library.'

'Let's see,' Charm said and moved to the nearest wall.

She stretched out her hand but stopped before touching the tapestry and instead reached for one of her short swords. Using the tip of the blade she lifted aside a layer of fabric to reveal a recess in the wall. 'As you see,' she said but Ciren frowned.

'Not books,' he pointed out, looking at the hoard of objects. 'These look like amulets . . .'

The shelf held eight black shards of obsidian, each attached to a leather cord. The twins looked at them, and then turned to look at each other, eyes travelling to the black talismans each wore around their neck.

'Translation amulets,' Ciren said, his voice failing. 'That's what they are.' His hand reached up to touch the obsidian amulet he wore and Charm grabbed his hand to stop him.

'Don't,' she said. 'Who knows what would happen if you broke the magic. Remember why we're here.'

Ciren nodded, although he was paler than ever, and his fingers pressed hers as they moved to the next wall. This time when Charm used her blade to lift aside the covering they were greeted with the sight they had expected.

The row of books was two shelves long, each volume bound in black and red and with the symbol of the Wheel set into the spine. But although they were superficially similar the resemblance ended with the covers. Along the line of books some were battered and scuffed, others warped by water damage or scorched by fire; a testament to the many missions the twins had undertaken for their patron. Charm picked up the last book on the shelf, the one they had turned over to Vespertine only the previous day, while Ciren picked up the first book instead.

Charm flicked through the last pages of the recent book, the rows of interchangeable script written by herself and her twin. Skimming back through the last events listed she paused over a particular line and read out loud.

*'Vespertine has made our duty clear. We go at his command to capture Morgan and Kal and bring them back to the Wheel.'* She flipped back and forward through the book before saying, 'After that we only wrote one-line entries, before it each entry lasted for pages.'

Ciren was still picking his way through the untidier scrawl of the first book and Charm put the one she was holding back, selecting another randomly.

'This one has the same pattern,' she said after a moment. 'The first few entries are short, but they become more detailed the longer we are away from Vespertine and the Wheel, including maps and sketches and essays on the places we have visited. Then we see Vespertine and the entries are a single line long: saying only what he has commanded us to do.'

Ciren raised his head from the book he was reading, with a grim expression.

'The first entry begins like this,' he said. *'Today Vespertine Chalcedony gave us this book. He has told us we must always write in it so that he will have a record of where we go and what we do and see. This is our duty as agents of the Wheel.'*

'Then it's always been like this. We've always done what Vespertine commanded,' Charm said.

Ciren turned to answer her and froze in place as a voice spoke calmly from behind them.

'Not always, my children. At times you have been most disobedient.'

# 10

When the trapdoor opened, Zoë didn't know if she was more relieved by the light or the anxious expression of Siffany as she stared down at them.

'I must beg your forgiveness,' she said straightaway, as she came down the stairs, looking them over with sudden solicitousness. 'The Wolves have standing orders to take no chances in the event of an alarm. I hope you were not injured, for the queen will take it ill if you were harmed in any way.'

'I'm OK,' Zoë said, ignoring the scrapes and bruises she had accumulated in her progress down the steep steps.

Laura was blinking in the light, her pale green eyes shifting disturbingly as she tried to compensate for her blindness, and Siffany came to help her up the stairs.

'What was the alarm?' Laura asked and Siffany gave her a thoughtful look.

'Your friend Jhezra was discovered spying on the

queen. But Lachesis forgave her and has said that you should be brought before her to hear what she will say to you all.'

'What she will say?' Zoë repeated, trying to make sense of Siffany's words. 'What will she say?'

'That you will soon discover,' Siffany pointed out, as they came up the stairs past two Wolves on guard and headed towards the throne room.

When they reached the door there were more guards, but they passed through unchallenged behind Siffany. Inside Lachesis was waiting, Lisle seated at her left hand side and Jhezra cross-legged on a cushion on the floor. The Hajhi girl looked up with relief at their entrance and Siffany nodded to her.

'Your companions are unharmed, although the Wolves had secluded them,' she said, with an air of pride.

'They appear to be in some disarray,' the queen said in her dry snap of a voice, glancing from Zoë to Laura. 'Have the Wolves mishandled you?' she demanded of them.

'Not really,' Zoë said. 'They just surprised me.' A hot blush rose up into her face as she remembered what they had surprised her doing and the queen looked amused.

'Still, we don't appreciate such treatment in a place where we were brought as guests,' Laura said sharply and Zoë forgot her blush in turning to glare at her.

'I shall make amends for any hurt you've suffered,' the queen announced. She turned to Jhezra and concluded, 'Sit and be at ease, and there shall be plain speaking between us.'

Zoë looked from Laura, who had found her way to a low stool and sat down, to Jhezra apparently at ease on her floor cushion.

'What . . . what about Kal?' she asked, looking back at the queen. 'He woke up, just before your Wolves threw us in jail. I was . . . with him.' She could feel herself blushing again, and her embarrassment was worse, knowing that the others could see it, but she shook off her awkwardness and appealed to Lisle. 'Shouldn't he be here as well, if you're going to tell us something important?'

'Perhaps . . .' Lisle turned to the queen, who looked towards Siffany.

'The boy who was sick,' Siffany said uncomfortably. 'I'm afraid there's a problem with him.'

The guards on duty at the entrance to the villa challenged Alex but let him pass when he displayed the note the barrack commander had given him. Walking up to the double doors he was surprised to find them open and the villa apparently deserted.

It was gloomy inside the villa; there were barely any windows and long hallways stretched back into the interior, covered with dark grey tapestries. Turning out of the main hall and walking down one of the long corridors the sound of boots on the marble floor was muted and weak. He heard nothing else as he came round a corner and suddenly saw Morgan standing in front of him.

She was staring into space but started back when he said her name, her eyes wide and surprised.

'It's me, Alex,' he said quickly. 'Are you all right?'

'Alex?' She still looked distracted, as if she didn't recognize him, and she looked behind him with so much alarm that he turned and looked back himself. There was nothing there, except the empty corridor.

'Morgan?' he said again, carefully, and waited until

her gaze tracked to meet his eyes. 'Do you remember me?'

'What are you doing here?' she said, her eyes narrowing with suspicion. 'Are you working for him?'

'What?' He shook his head as he tried to understand what she was talking about. 'If you mean the Wheel, I haven't exactly had much choice. I was kidnapped here the same as you were, remember? They've had me doing basic training with their soldiers at the fort up on the hill.'

'Then you are working for him,' she said. 'For Vespertine Chalcedony. The leader of the Wheel.'

Alex hesitated for a second but he didn't like the look she was giving him and he spoke hurriedly to reassure her.

'Give me a break, Morgan,' he said. 'I might not be your favourite person but I'm not a megalomaniac. You know, I was worried about you. I wasn't sure what those two were planning when they dragged you off.'

'They were working for Vespertine,' Morgan said, returning to the subject obsessively. But her face had softened from its rigid focus and she was looking for the first time as if she knew him. 'He wants me to work for him, the way they do, but I won't.' She wrung her hands in a nervous gesture, like the goth girl he remembered, and repeated almost frantically, 'I won't.'

'OK, steady on,' Alex told her. 'You realize this world is full of Wheel agents, right. You can't exactly cut and run that easily.'

'Can't I?' Morgan's green eyes met his with the most alarming look she'd given yet and he wondered if her problems had finally driven her insane. 'I'm going to try though. Kal and I escaped the Wheel once before. I can do it again.'

Alex glanced up and down the corridor but there was

no one in sight. It seemed unlikely that they'd just be able to walk away, especially if this Vespertine Chalcedony wanted Morgan to stay. But he remembered the power of the spell she'd cast on Laura and looked back at her with a new respect.

'You're going to use your magic to escape?' he said and when she nodded, made a quick decision. 'Then I'm coming with you.'

Her eyes narrowed in suspicion but then she shook herself and shrugged.

'Whatever,' she said. 'Just don't try to stop me.' Then added with a vicious edge in her voice, 'I mean it, Alex Harrell. You'd better be on my side this time.'

'No problem,' he said and even sketched a salute. Morgan might be acting like a nutcase but he realized he had absolutely no desire to meet the person who had made her like this. 'Let's go. The door's this way . . .'

He started to turn and stopped, as Morgan's eyes widened enormously. He'd always thought it was just a metaphor but he could feel his skin actually crawling as he turned to look at what she had seen.

Kal didn't know how long he'd been sitting there when a middle-aged man in plain clothes opened the door.

Unlike the guards who had restrained him earlier, this man stood for a moment inside the doorway, allowing Kal to get a good look at him before moving with slow unthreatening steps into the room. Once he was inside, the door shut behind him and he spoke, his voice low, calm, and controlled.

Kal looked back at him uncomprehendingly. To his ears the words meant nothing. The man could have been expressing concern, but he equally might have been chanting a poetic saga or asking what Kal was doing in his bedchamber. Without the translation magic of the Archon's crown, Kal could do no more than guess.

'Forgive me,' Kal said. The memory of his own actions earlier weighed heavily on him and he met the man's eyes openly, trying to express something of his remorse in the tone of his voice. 'I do not understand your speech.'

The newcomer frowned and spoke again, his voice questioning this time. As the man came closer, Kal tried to smile in apology but his expression felt wrong.

'Forgive me,' he said again.

The low voice spoke again, gently. With a careful gesture, the man pointed to himself and said, 'Usher.' Then he took the wrapped cloth he had carried into the room with him and, laying it on the bed, unrolled it to display gleaming tools, with delicate blades and prongs. Each was tucked into a loop or pocket to hold it in place. 'Maedthurndlar,' he said, pointing to the tools and then to himself.

'Kal.' Copying the man's gesture Kal pointed to himself and then looked at the tools again. They could have been used for almost any craft. For woodcarving, tailoring, or book binding. But no one from those trades would be sent to speak with a sick stranger and Kal could guess what the man was trying to say. 'You are a healer?'

'Maedthurndlar,' the man called Usher said again and followed this with more foreign words. 'Hardth scurdthlakenihr til lachesis. Ehrg er hihr til jhalfa thu.'

Kal concentrated but could understand nothing of this and lifted his hands in a gesture of incomprehension. The healer stopped speaking and reached out slowly, locking his gaze with Kal's as he closed his fingers around Kal's wrists. Kal looked down at his hands as the man drew his gaze to them and saw them bloody with small cuts where he had gripped the crown.

Usher released him and went to the side of the room where another leather roll lay next to packets and small jars and boxes. Taking one of the boxes and a strip of clean linen he brought them back to Kal and showed them to him before reaching out a hand with a questioning look.

'Thank you,' Kal said. As the healer cleaned his cuts and salved them before binding each hand in a section of linen he asked, 'Was it you who removed the crown?' He accompanied the question with a gesture of his free hand towards Usher, then to the crown and mimed the act of lifting from his head.

'Fyhrgeyfa maeg.' The man nodded once and made a gesture to his chest and then towards Kal that meant nothing. But the expression in his eyes seemed to speak of apology and Kal smiled grimly.

'I should thank you,' he said. 'But since we do not speak each other's tongue and I don't know what has brought me here or why your cure was effective . . .' he paused. 'My speech is worthless.'

The healer seemed to have decided something similar himself. When he had finished binding Kal's hands he rolled up his instruments and stood, taking a step backwards before pointing to the door, then himself and Kal and tilting his head slightly before speaking in a tone of request.

'Faljha thu kommar org taller meag drortnang lachesis?'

'As you wish.' Kal stood. He had no idea where the man intended to lead him but there were no answers to be found in this room.

It had been a long time since Kal thought of himself as the Archon of Shattershard but now, as he followed the surgeon through the interlinked rooms of the building, it was as if his city had never fallen. The world he walked through seemed pale and flimsy compared to the images that had haunted his dreams. As if a door had been unlocked, he felt the power of the Archon's crown whispering through the corridors of his mind.

They reached a door guarded by two soldiers who stood aside as the surgeon knocked. A woman, dressed in the same uniform, opened it from the other side and stepped back to let him enter. A group of people sat by a wide fireplace in the room beyond and Kal looked from one to the other of them. The woman at the centre wore the dress of a queen and so it was to her he finally spoke.

'Was it by your order, lady, that I was brought to this place against my will?'

Morgan felt it before she saw it, a building pressure, like vertigo or claustrophobia or trying to move in a dream when your body seemed made of lead. The *something* she'd been afraid of, behind Vespertine Chalcedony's soothing words, had crept out from wherever it had been hiding and even the air around her seemed infused with a horrible and insistent menace. Someone was casting a spell.

Alex had jerked backwards as if he could feel it too but when she saw the bewilderment on his face she realized he didn't understand at all.

'We have to get out. Now.' Morgan tried to run in the direction he'd indicated and felt the nightmare become real as time seemed to slow down.

The grey tapestries were billowing out from the walls, the complicated loops and swirls of embroidery floating into the air and netting thin strands from wall to wall.

'Oh, good God,' Alex said in a queer voice and he wrenched at the sword at his waist, swearing to himself as he tried to free it.

'It's a spell,' Morgan said, hearing her own voice come thinly as she reached out to tear at the webbed strands in front of her. The network was becoming thicker, the distances shading to a darker grey as the thread-like strands began to fill the corridor. 'The whole villa, we have to get out . . .'

'No kidding,' Alex said, finally freeing the sword and hacking at the strands, slicing them free so that they curled and looped in the air like Medusa's snakes. Brandishing the sword in his right hand he groped for her with his left and she grabbed hold of him.

Laura's blurred vision had strained to read Kal's expression as he entered the room but all she could make out was the pale haze of his face and hair above the dark blur of his clothing. His first words were antagonistic, bitingly cold as he addressed the queen.

'Was it by your order, lady, that I was brought to this place against my will?'

Laura kept silent, dropping her gaze to look at the ground. She'd never known much about Kal back in the days when she and Alex had been planning to overthrow him from the throne of Shattershard. She'd had nothing particularly against him but he'd always seemed a vague and ineffectual kind of ruler. Now she heard the grim confidence in his voice, the attitude of someone who was never questioned, and she felt ill-at-ease. If Kal blamed her for what had happened to Morgan, and he might well, she doubted she'd be able to talk fast enough to save herself.

Squinting sideways she tried to see if he was wearing a sword and almost missed the queen's response.

'I cannot understand what he says.' She turned to Lisle with raised eyebrows. 'Yet he appears angry.'

Siffany moved closer, a hand going to her own weapon, but Lisle waved her back.

'My queen cannot understand your speech,' she said to Kal. 'But I wear a charm that should allow my words to be translated to you. It was I who caused you to be brought here that the spell which held you powerless might be broken.'

'Then I owe you my thanks,' Kal said, although his voice was still suspicious. 'But in removing the Archon's crown I lack the magics that allow my words to be translated.'

Laura found herself smiling at Lisle's response. The older woman seemed so sophisticated in her understanding of the Library and the Collegiate but she'd obviously not anticipated this translation problem and there was a pause while she sent a servant to fetch another charm from her pack. Laura wondered why the queen had no amulet of her own but speculated that in a world where magic was so weak the politicians hadn't got into the habit of using magic, as the ones in Shattershard had.

During the delay Kal obviously took the opportunity to study their group and Laura saw his face turn to look at each of them in turn. Jhezra made some gesture of greeting when Kal looked at her, but Zoë fidgeted and looked away. Laura lifted her head to look at the Archon and for a moment she seemed to meet those cold grey eyes before he turned away.

The servant returned at a run and Lisle passed the amulet to Kal. Lifting it over his head, he nodded his thanks and then spoke the words that Laura could have predicted.

'If I was brought here what happened to Morgan?'

There was an uncomfortable pause and then Lisle replied in a carefully gentle voice, 'You were present for the judgement of the court. When you were incapacitated it was carried out.'

'You let the Wheel take her?' Kal said, his voice rising in anger. 'When we warned you what they were like?'

'I regret I had no power to stop them,' Lisle replied. 'By the rules of the Collegiate they were counted as fit guardians. But two Jurists were sent to make sure justice was done.'

'Justice.' Kal's voice rang with sarcasm. 'The Wheel want Morgan's magic to conquer worlds, and you call it *justice* to hand her back to them? Is everyone in your Collegiate so blind to the truth?'

'So it has often seemed to me,' came the dry voice of Queen Lachesis and Laura found herself craning her neck to listen, certain that if Kal would only shut up for a minute they would hear the secrets Lisle had kept from them about her past.

'We are all blind,' Lisle said and her tones mingled bitterness and despair. 'We stumble from Door to Door looking for something to lighten our darkness.'

A hush fell over the room and as Lisle continued to speak, Laura realized that the queen was no longer the primary force in the room, if indeed she ever had been. Thinking back to history lessons on the English monarchy, Laura thought she understood. Kings and queens might be powerful but there were lords and councillors more powerful still, people who manipulated politics to get the kind of ruler they wanted without ever stepping into the limelight themselves. People like Warwick and Walsingham and the Howards; they stayed in the shadows and were called kingmakers, because by their actions kings were crowned or brought down.

Kal must have decided that this was something he wanted to hear because he stilled in place, not sitting, but no longer radiating the kind of tension that suggested he might go berserk at any moment. Laura opened her eyes as wide as she could to stare across the room and make out the figure of Siffany, standing guarding the queen, but her attention shifted to her mother.

'I pretend to no wisdom, nor to any altruism. I have only ever done what seemed best to me. Will you hear my story? I promise it will not take long.'

'Speak,' Kal said. And as he gave his permission it seemed for a moment that it was he and not the queen who was the real ruler here.

'I was born on this world in a marcher barony. Fenrisnacht is a harsh place, unforgiving and relentless, but back then we had more to fear than the storms of snow and ice. Men ruled here, men like Wutan.'

A shadow seemed to pass over them as Siffany moved closer to her mother and the queen turned her head away to stare into the dark corners of the room.

'We women worked as hard as any man, tending the hearth-fires of our poor homes, keeping warmth and hope alive through the long winters. But for all our work, nothing we made was ours, not even our selves. We were the possession of our fathers or husbands, who might do as they chose with us, and when I displeased the baron he cast me out.'

'Into the snow?' Zoë's voice was thin and frightened and Lisle's reply was quieter still.

'Into the snow. There my story would have ended were it not for the Door I stumbled across. A Door that led into the Library.'

Laura thought about that, of what that change would have meant to a girl her own age, oppressed by a culture that allowed her nothing for herself. She'd seen the effect of such a transition on Morgan, Zoë, and Jhezra, all of whom had benefited from the knowledge of other worlds. But none of them had been brutalized by their home world as much as Lisle had been.

In the quiet room the old woman's voice continued, gaining strength as she told them how she'd come to join the Collegiate.

'The Woodcarvers then were a little like the Jurists today, the difference being that they kept the rules themselves but did not enforce them on others. They took me in and taught me about the Library and while I travelled to other worlds where the sun shone and I might do as I pleased I thought I would never return home.'

'It was fortunate for us that you did,' the queen said softly.

'So I think,' Lisle said with a flash of humour in her voice. 'But I should not have done so had I not fallen in with a faction that my benefactors thought dangerous.'

'The Lightbringers,' someone said and Laura realized it was her.

'Yes,' Lisle admitted. 'A faction that bent the rules of interference and supported me when I realized I wanted to come back here and free my sisters from the tyranny of Wutan's men.' She looked from Laura to Jhezra as she added, 'Our rebellion was not so different from yours, though we had neither magic nor machines of war. We used only our knowledge of strategies and tactics to mobilize our army of women. But in the end that was enough.'

'Library learning made me a queen,' Lachesis said ironically. 'But Collegiate custom called my counsellors renegades.'

'And so we were,' Lisle agreed, but she sounded proud and her voice had gained strength as she told them about the Lightbringers. 'After Fenrisnacht we used our strength to bring a similar freedom to many other worlds. Never for glory, but we gained glory just the same. In the end we angered too many factions. Those that saw us as rule-breakers and those who would have broken yet more laws without our restraining influence. Somehow our secrets were discovered and our faction discredited throughout the Library.'

'If you stood so far outside the law, what were you doing working with the Jurists?' Kal asked, voicing his suspicions in a way that reminded Laura not to underestimate him.

'People forget,' Lisle said simply. 'I spent many years here, travelling only rarely and in disguise. I had three children and built up the province that was my father's. When my first daughter was old enough to care for my holdings I came back to the Library and discovered the name Lisle Weft was long forgotten.'

Lisle paused in her story and sighed before coming to her conclusion, one that Laura was beginning to suspect.

'Among the Jurists I tried to honour the law as the Woodcarvers had done when I was too young to appreciate their work. I tried and failed and you have seen what that faction has become. When you arrived I remembered a warning brought by an old friend, that a new time of trouble was coming for all the worlds, at the hands of the faction that calls itself the Wheel.' Lisle looked around, at each of them in turn. 'Against this danger strict adherence to the law is not enough and there are no Lightbringers to fight them. At least not yet.'

Ciren had seen the fear on the faces of rebels as they realized the Wheel knew their secrets. The looks they'd given him and his twin, while being taken away for punishment, had been like that of a trapped animal that knows itself utterly at your mercy.

But there had been no mercy for the rebels. Ciren understood that now; there was no place for it in Vespertine Chalcedony's world.

'Did you think I would not notice when my children ceased to trust me?' the founder of the Wheel asked with appalling gentleness, as he faced them across the room. 'You have betrayed so many, it was inevitable that you would turn against me.'

Ciren wondered if it was deliberate on his patron's part that they should sense the magic cresting and know their powers would be useless to stop it. It rose around him like a grey mist, a complex network of spells prepared for this purpose, spells to bind and snare and trap. They coiled out of the walls and floors and from the crooked figure of Vespertine Chalcedony, flowing from the folds of his cloak. It was a magic he knew he'd sensed before, fogging his mind and returning him to his duty as an agent of Vespertine's will.

His one slim hope of escape lay with his twin, that she would have thought of a way to save them from this. He turned to her and felt his heart stall suddenly at the terrible smile that stretched her lips.

'There will be no escape,' she said and he realized with another jolt it was not his mind she was reading but their master's. 'If we outlive our usefulness there is a replacement prepared.'

'Morgan won't do what you want,' Ciren said, thinking of a way out and quailed as Vespertine's magic surged again.

'She will,' he told them. 'It is unfortunate that I did not acquire her as young as I did you. But she understands her power even less than you did. You can be sure she will make a fitting vessel for mine.'

'A slave,' Charm said, and Ciren didn't know if she spoke her own thoughts or Vespertine's. 'Her magic subjugated to yours.'

'How else am I to accomplish my great mission?' Vespertine enquired, his tones still perfectly reasonable. 'But do not be afraid, my children. You have not quite yet outlived your usefulness to me.'

His grey robes flowed back, carrying him a pace away from the open doorway and he raised a hand to gesture them forward.

'Come,' he said. 'I always listen to your warnings. If Morgan is not convinced by rational argument you shall make her more amenable to my will.'

# 11

Looking past the glow of the fire to the stone room Jhezra saw the black sky visible through the open window. The stars were scattered across this sky as well, and she wondered if each star was a world, and the Library the darkness in between.

Within their fire-lit circle the others were silent, occupied with their own thoughts as Lisle finished her story. Laura's head was bent forward, her expression hidden by the smooth brown curtain of her hair. Zoë was frowning into the fire, her expression full of uncertainty and fear. Lisle watched them with the same shrewd assessment she had given them all at one time or another and Siffany watched her mother as if trying to comprehend everything Lisle was and had been.

But the queen, Lachesis, was watching Kal. He stood on the edge of their circle, shadows shifting across his grey eyes like storm clouds.

'When I first discovered the Doors,' Kal spoke and

they all turned to look at him, 'it was because others had come to my world with the intention of using it to gain power.' His gaze flickered towards Laura for an instant. 'And I would think the laws of the Collegiate good, were it not that I have seen how easily they may be broken. The Wheel used the fall of my city to consolidate their power over my world.' He paused and turned to look at Jhezra, adding, 'Our world.'

'I don't blame the Jurists for judging us,' Jhezra replied. 'But I have thought for some time now that they knew too little to judge wisely. If what you have learnt and Lisle suspects of the Wheel is true then I cannot think of a Collegiate faction that can stand in their way.' She took a breath and then looked to Lisle as she asked, 'You said the Lightbringers are gone. Is it your hope to recreate them, perhaps with us the first of your army?'

'You see too clearly for my comfort,' Lisle admitted. 'But in truth, I'm done with armies. I may not be wiser now but I'm older and that's close enough. I've told Zoë a little of what I plan to do.'

'You said you would ask Caravaggion's advice,' Zoë said, mentioning the mysterious figure whose name seemed to have shadowed them during their travels.

'On the world of Mandarel, ten Doors stand in a ring,' said Lisle. 'Each leads to a different section of the Library. The people who live there are neither world-dwellers nor world-travellers and even when I first met them they set a standard for enlightenment. Now, as the Collegiate slides into a Dark Age, the Mandela stands virtually alone as a bastion of true knowledge. That is where I will travel now to seek help against the Wheel.'

'Would someone there know how to lift the curse on me?' Laura asked and as Lisle was about to speak Kal turned to stare at her.

'A curse you have used to your advantage,' he said, slicing off his words abruptly. 'The rest of these people I hold no ill will towards but I have unfinished business with you.'

'Leaving Laura aside,' Lisle managed to draw their attention back to her, 'it seems that your quarrel is with the Wheel.'

'With the Wheel and perhaps with the Collegiate,' Kal said and nodded towards the queen. 'It seems your majesty's involvement with world-travellers has been more fortunate than mine. But I doubt the wisdom of allowing the people of this world to remain ignorant of Doors. It seems to me that while the Collegiate rules are unclear it falls to those who dwell on the worlds to set a standard for those who travel them.'

'An interesting thought,' the queen said slowly. 'But I should fear the effect on our nation if too many were lured away by the hope of a better future on another world.'

'In either case those who control access to the Doors control access to worlds,' Kal said and Jhezra nodded to herself.

'It seems to me that you were right to break the Library laws to serve your people. I would do the same for mine. The Wheel control access to my world and they also have a Door to Earth,' she said out loud, looking from Kal to Zoë and Laura. 'If this Mandela Lisle describes has some idea how to combat them I should like to know what it is.'

'I'll go too,' Zoë said softly. 'Though I think Kal might be right that it would be better to let people back home know about the Collegiate so that they can prepare. But perhaps the Mandela Doors might lead to a way back to Earth?'

'Perhaps,' Lisle said. 'Although I make no promises.'

She turned to look from Laura to Kal. 'And what of you two? What will you do?'

'I will come to the Mandela,' Kal said, ignoring Laura. 'But I also make no promises as to what I may do beyond that. I have my own ideas as to how to combat the Wheel. We will see if they sit well with those of your allies.'

There was a pause as Kal fell silent, still ignoring Laura while the rest of them waited for her answer. Jhezra thought to herself that this might be a place Laura would actually want to stay. Here at least she had glimmerings of sight, and there might be an opportunity for her to work her political manipulations from within the queen's court. She wondered if Lisle was thinking the same thing.

'I'd like to see this ring of Doors,' Laura told them, lifting her head in Lisle's direction. 'But can I? If it is a place of powerful magic it sounds as if I'll be blind again.' Suddenly she shifted to look straight at Kal, her green eyes wide and defenceless. 'And can I come if the Archon here still holds a grudge against me? If blindness isn't enough of a punishment, what will satisfy you?'

Laura was using her weakness as a weapon again, Jhezra realized, the same defence she'd adopted for the Jurists and the one she used to run rings around herself and Zoë. But Kal considered her with distaste.

'No punishment,' he said curtly. 'And if I find Morgan again I'll find a way for her to recall the spell she cast. But I could wish no worse fate upon you than understanding the truth of what you have done. Pray that you never do.'

The moment he'd realized that Morgan really did have magic had stood out in Alex's mind. At one time he'd thought the Doors Between Worlds were something that could be scientifically quantified. Morgan's magic had brought his plans crashing down, literally, and ever since he'd been consumed by the question of how you could operate on an equal footing with other world-travellers when magic could be brought into play.

The spell on the villa showed him how right he'd been to fear it. As the threads webbed the corridor he used the only weapon he had, slashing his sword right and left to make a path for them. But the cut threads curved around and back again, collecting around his sword and trying to cocoon it with gluey strands.

Alex cursed under his breath as he fought to free it, and managed to hack a large enough space for him to pull Morgan around the corner of the corridor.

'Lucky I'm not arachnophobic,' he said, glancing at Morgan, and wished he hadn't. She looked worse than when she'd been in the fugue state, her eyes glittering wildly and her hands fumbling and twisting the empty air in front of her. Odds were she *was* scared of spiders and he reminded himself not to say anything that would set her off. 'So how's about some of the old mojo?' he said, trying to jolt her into action. 'I don't think there'll be a better time than this.'

'I'm trying,' she said, and it was a surprise to realize she'd actually heard him. 'But Vespertine's spell is old, and powerful. It's more than just the tapestries, it's all through this house and this world, pouring out of his mind . . .'

Her words became less coherent and Alex gritted his teeth, wondering if being a magician also meant you had to be mental.

'So how about something to cut through the crap?' he asked, looking down the hall ahead, now festooned with the cobwebby traces of magic dropping from the ceiling and building up from the floor as well as stringing from wall to wall around them. 'Come on, Morgan. I can't do this all on my own . . .'

'Something to cut the cords, break the tie . . .' she muttered to herself and then grinned fiercely. '*Yes.*'

Morgan raised her hands, her thin fingers crooked at an unpleasant angle, her face pulled back tautly into a grimace like a hissing cat. Alex dodged back as she stabbed her hands forward, unleashing a rippling tide of blackness that engulfed the greyness ahead. Alex turned in time to see the tapestry cobwebs melting from the walls, crumbling away as the black wave rolled through them.

'Holy hellfire,' he said, awed, before realizing the way was now clear. 'Let's go.'

Morgan was standing stock still, her eyes wide as she stared in front of her, and Alex shook his head, grabbing her by one trailing sleeve of her gown and pulling her along with him. Once he'd got her moving she broke into a run and they pelted down the corridor through the tunnel the black flame had created.

They pelted out into the main hall and into a surprisingly open space. Alex had time to take in the fact that the tapestries had crawled to cover the double doors of the entrance before skidding to a halt. Ciren and Charm were standing in the middle of the room, and a little behind them a grey figure in a hooded cloak stood with his hands on their shoulders.

'Most impressive,' he said. 'For a novice. Now shall we see what my apprentices can do?'

Morgan flinched back from the man, almost hiding behind Alex, and his hand tightened on the hilt of his sword as he realized this was the person she was afraid of.

'And who are you?' he demanded. 'Darth Vader?'

'Strange words from one who wears my insignia,'

the cloaked figure replied with an edge of menace in his voice. But Alex was already as terrified as it was possible to be and his tongue seemed to roll on before him.

'I guess the zombie twins here didn't get round to mentioning me,' he said. 'Your goons up on the hill have been filling me in on your plans for world domination and I've decided I'd rather pass.'

'Who is this fool?' the magician demanded and Charm fixed Alex with a sneering smile.

'A child in a man's body,' she said. 'Fear carries him to heights of boldness he would not dare to face with sanity. He's no threat to you, master.'

'Morgan's magic falters,' Ciren continued in the same dead monotone. 'She cannot conserve her strength and she has already expended much of her energy on breaking free of the spell knots.'

'What are you, the narrator?' Alex snarled. Charm's cool assessment of him had spurred him on to a height of fury and whatever they thought of him he still had a weapon in his hand.

Fear kept in place for a moment longer, then with a yell he charged at Ciren, swinging the sword. Dishonourable it might be since the boy's only weapon was the bow he carried on his back but he'd already seen what Charm could do with her blades and he didn't want to get close to the sinister figure that must be Vespertine Chalcedony.

'Narrate this!' he shouted. And as he ran forward he heard Morgan give a strangled choke of laughter.

Ciren saw the blow coming but the grey fog of Vespertine's magic that filled his mind would not let him move. He had time to think it might be better if Alex did cut him down, at least then there might be an end to his betrayals.

Alex's rapier met Charm's short sword with a grating screech as she leapt to the defence. As she blocked the strike with her left sword arm, she drew her other blade and levelled it at the Earth boy. Still frozen in place and feeling Vespertine's claw-like hand gripping his shoulder, Ciren realized his twin had more freedom of movement than he did and wondered if it was because she'd always been more willing to let their patron overshadow her mind. But the blank dead look in her purple eyes didn't infect him with the fear it had at the lake. He knew what expression his own face must be wearing as Vespertine Chalcedony used them to bring Morgan into the same servitude they had endured for years unknowingly.

Alex's movement had set something free in Morgan; straightening out of the cringing stance of an animal at bay, she shook her head back and looked at Vespertine with jungle-green eyes.

'Alex was right,' she said. 'Your script is tired.' Her words spilled out in the same uncontrollable flood she had used to berate the twins. 'There's no way you're making me like them,' she continued and added incomprehensibly: 'And real Goths aren't scared of spiders.'

Black lightning crackled around her fingers as she raised her hands.

'You were right too,' she told Vespertine. 'I don't know what I'm doing. So really . . . this might do *anything*!'

The last word was screamed as she released her spell and sent it crackling and flaming across the space between them. From behind Ciren a grey fog writhed out to meet it, and shadow descended across the room as the spells collided with a boom of unsound.

Swords clanged again from the shadows in front of

him but it was no longer possible to make out the details of Charm and Alex's conflict. Ciren felt Vespertine's power grip his mind, squeezing it to force the use of his magic.

'My master's spell tightens but Morgan has found a new source of strength,' he recited obediently. 'Black fire caged in rock, hidden beneath the Earth, her need calls and channels it . . . imprisoned magic set free . . .'

For the second time on this world he felt the power of that magic overtake him, drawing him deeper into trance. He struggled, fighting both it and Vespertine, and then abruptly relaxed, and allowed the mingled magics to swamp him, falling back into the strength of it and letting it overtake his mind. Vespertine's hand released him with a twitch of displeasure but Ciren was beyond consciousness now: nothing but a mouthpiece for the magic. From a distance he could hear his own voice raving, and hoped against hope that Morgan would understand.

'Black shards of rock, the magics that collar and choke, they chain the magic but it can be loosed. A grey net covers it, but Morgan's tears the cobwebs from the locked doors, opening the way. The tower trembles on the black crag, the fortress guards from inside . . . I feel the black wheel spinning in the sky . . .'

Charm parried and blocked, parried and blocked, forcing Alex back and herself further away from Vespertine. From the wild look in Alex's eyes it was clear he thought he was fighting for his life, and she didn't allow herself to think of anything except reading his ripostes. Vespertine's magic was still spiralling in and out of her mind but on a looser leash than it might have been.

Vespertine had always been more certain of her than Ciren, certain of her unquestioning obedience of his orders. Even now he kept only enough of a hold to be sure of her.

As Ciren's words came freely as he fell deeper into trance, she realized what her twin was doing. He had opened himself to the magic, his power open for Morgan to use it as well as their patron.

With that realization Charm felt her smile expand. Alex flinched back, but she cared little for what he thought. Expanding her consciousness to include the crackling intensity of Morgan's mind and the grey sink that was Vespertine's.

'Charm opens her mind, and the channel flows backwards. The cloud falls before the flame and the key turns in the lock.' Charm could feel her own magic connecting and meshing with Ciren's and by extension Vespertine's, as she rode the wave of Morgan's black fire to break through the locks Vespertine had used to chain their memory. As the missing parts of her mind were filled she heard Ciren give a sharp cry of pain and shout, 'I fall backwards out of the web and through the Door . . . into the past.'

She remembered that Door, remembered a life behind it like a distant dream, and then arriving through the inside-out tower to feel the weight of Vespertine's chains come down upon her neck.

Her swords had faltered in their weaving patch as she released her magic and in a blur she saw Alex step through her defence, sword raised. But as her muscles jerked into action she knew that he was no longer trying to kill her, even as his free hand reached out for her neck.

'Defend yourself!' she heard Vespertine demand, too late. Alex's hand clawed frantically at her throat for an instant before he grabbed the cord of her amulet and ripped it free, sending a slice of pain whipping across the back of her neck.

The grey fog in Charm's mind thinned into a mist and she came crashing to her knees on the floor at the sudden release from Vespertine's thrall. Morgan's magic was in the ascendance now. Charm saw dimly that Alex had turned to Ciren and was reaching with a strangler's grip for him through the thick black cloud that had enveloped their master.

As Alex tore Ciren's amulet off, the boy twin fell forward, and Alex dragged him stumbling back towards Morgan. As he did so the cloud that had surrounded Vespertine and with it the shadows in the room, fell apart, and incongruously Charm saw pale sunlight shining through the open doors. But Vespertine still stood, facing Morgan across the room, his posture as still as a snake about to strike. Charm stared up at him, realizing for the first time that under the white rheum his eyes were the same purple-black as her own.

Vespertine's hands groped the empty air in front of him and his head turned sharply from side to side, looking for them.

'The spell you cast on Laura,' Alex said, panting for breath. 'You've blinded him.'

'I cursed him . . .' Morgan whispered. 'I still don't know how.' She was looking down at the twisting fingers of her hands.

''Ware Vespertine,' Charm warned as the cloaked figure turned to focus on Morgan once more. Alex lifted his sword but stilled again as beneath their feet the grey flagstones of the floor began to tremble.

'It's not over . . .' Ciren gasped from his fallen position and Charm pushed herself upright, reaching to pull her twin up with her.

The tapestries were gone but the pale grey stone of the villa was shifting and warping, dark grey veins appearing in the smooth surface and thickening as they spread across the room.

'You have not the faintest conception of my power,' Vespertine whispered, as the shadows began to return from the corners, in a voice like dead leaves scudding in the wind. 'What are your curses to me? I never needed eyes to see . . .'

Morgan heard Vespertine's words with weary desperation. She'd used all the power she could find and it was not enough. But, for the second time, Alex was the one to jolt her out of despair.

'Then don't wait for him to blast us!' he shouted, shaking her loose of her terror. 'RUN!'

Charm and Ciren were already stumbling towards the door, supporting each other. The veins in the marble were running down the walls and across the floor, opening like dark cracks beneath her feet and Morgan needed no more prompting. Jumping the cracks she caught up with Alex and they pushed the twins with them out into the watery sunlight.

Fish were still swimming in the rectangular pond, Morgan noticed as they ran past.

'Horses,' Ciren gasped, flinging out an arm to point, and Alex replied:

'Good idea . . .'

Somehow they were all on the same side now and Morgan wondered if it was hypocritical to feel a sense of relief about that; that she was no longer facing Vespertine alone. She could still feel the grey magic swelling in the back of her mind and knew that they hadn't bought themselves much time.

As they arrived around the side of the villa at the stables, Charm pushed Ciren towards Morgan, as she and Alex ran towards the stalls. Morgan struggled to support Ciren's weight as he slumped against her, and could only watch as Charm grabbed a kind of halter and buckled it around one horse's neck.

'Here,' she called, throwing Alex an identical halter and nodding towards another horse. 'No time for saddles.'

'Agreed,' Alex replied, sheathing his sword and hastening to harness the second horse.

'I'm not much of a rider,' Morgan admitted.

'Now would be a good time to get better,' Charm said curtly, leading her own horse out. As she came towards Morgan she glanced at her twin and asked, 'Ciren, can you ride?'

'I think so,' Ciren said, but he looked ill and Charm came round to take his arm and help boost him up on to the horse, swinging herself up behind him and leaning around her twin's body to take the reins. Even riding bareback she looked confident and Morgan looked uneasily at the horse Alex was leading out.

Still, she'd done this once before, escaping from Shattershard. Alex helped her mount and struggled on behind her, as the grey stone of the villa began to churn, as if it were mouldering away.

'Which way?' Alex shouted, as Charm kicked her horse forward. 'The Door will be guarded . . .'

'There's another Door,' Ciren managed to say, lifting his head to look across at them. 'The one . . . we came through . . . our world . . .'

'Vespertine stole our memories, but now they return,' Charm explained, urging them out of the gate and on to the road, pointing towards a ridge of wooded hillside in the distance. 'He tried to hide the Door but your magic unlocked the past. Behind it lies something he fears so much his thoughts are clouded.'

'There's an expression,' Alex said, out loud. 'Your enemy's enemy is your friend.'

'Succinct,' Charm said drily, looking around their party as they rode out on to the road. 'And appropriate in the circumstances.'

A tiny smile still creased her lips but Morgan didn't fear it, in this situation it might be better to have someone who responded to your thoughts instead of whatever you managed to articulate of them.

'Morgan,' Ciren said. 'You decide . . . which way?'

'The twins' Door,' she said immediately, her mind revolting from the idea of going back into the Library, through those miles of corridors owned by the Wheel. Who knew what spells he might conjure to trap them or what resources he had yet to call upon? 'Vespertine's putting out half his energy to keep it closed,' she said. 'Whatever lies on the other side he'd do anything to stop us reaching it.'

'Then that's the way we go,' Alex agreed and the horses lurched into an alarmingly fast pace, jolting her as they sped up the road towards the hills.

Zoë thought they might have waited, and indeed the queen had offered them the choice to spend the night in the Winter Palace. But Kal's eyes had glittered with an unnatural light when he said, 'I have slept long enough.'

Siffany sent the Wolves to prepare the sleds and Lisle went to retrieve her dog from the kennels. Laura and Jhezra slipped off to collect their possessions and doubtless to discuss the result of their plotting and Zoë was left alone with Kal.

She didn't know what to say so she said nothing, and fiddled nervously with a wooden bowl that stood on a sideboard. It was filled with smooth swirled stones, transparent ribbons of blue and green running through the rock. Letting them trickle through her fingers, she heard Kal speak and the blood thundered in her ears making it hard to hear him.

' . . . to ask you . . .' he was saying.

'Sorry . . .' Zoë said, turning around to look at him. 'What were you saying?'

'I wanted to ask you,' Kal said, grey eyes seeming to coolly assess her, 'what you are doing travelling the worlds like this? I seem to remember that you told the Jurists you wanted to return home?'

'I did . . . I do,' Zoë stammered. 'But the Jurists, they sent Alex and. . . Morgan back to Earth. Except that the Wheel agents were supposed to be taking them there. I heard what you and . . . Morgan said about them and I didn't trust them.'

Each reiteration of Morgan's name made her chest feel as if it was trapped in a vice, knowing how obsessed Kal was with her and in what desperate trouble she might be now. The imprint of that kiss seemed to be burned on to her mouth like a brand, a sign she had done something unforgivable. And worse was the fact that Kal was acting as if it hadn't happened at all. The words he wasn't saying seemed to block out the ones he spoke:

'So I see one person believed us,' he said. 'I wonder . . .'

'Yes?' Zoë held her breath.

'Do you know what happened to my sword? I had it in the Library but it wasn't in my room when I awoke.'

He spoke so matter-of-factly, not faltering at all, that Zoë felt her own ineptness stand out more obviously.

'I don't know,' she said, and felt the blush creeping up to her face again, turning away before he could see it. 'I'll ask.'

'Zoë . . .' Kal took a step forward and she waited. 'It is Zoë, isn't it?'

'Yes.'

'Thank you.'

She shrugged her shoulders, trying to shake loose her discomfort.

'It's nothing,' she said.

'Not for that.' He smiled slightly. 'For waking me.'

She stared at him and felt the blush hot on her face. Ducking her head, she turned around and headed for the door.

'It was nothing,' she said again.

# 12

The landscape around them still looked normal as Alex and the others rode towards the hills. But Morgan and the twins looked around at the neat shapes of farms and buildings with suspicion, twisting around to see if anything was coming after them.

Charm reined in her horse as the road passed a wood and then cantered it forward to jump the fence, Ciren clinging on limply to the reins. Morgan, holding the reins of their horse, managed to rein it in but then it stood sideways on to the fence and she asked a little wildly, 'How do you get it to jump?'

Turning around to watch them, Charm saw the problem and called out, 'Can you do it?'

'Here,' Alex said, reaching his arms around Morgan to take the reins, and kicking the horse into a turn. It wasn't easy riding bareback with only the most rudimentary halter and no bit or bridle. But he managed to do it and Morgan sucked in her breath sharply as they jumped the fence. 'You haven't ridden much, have you?' he said as they cantered after the twins' horse.

'When would I have got the chance in Weybridge?' Morgan said, through gritted teeth, slipping and sliding on the horse as she clung on to the reins with a death-grip. 'And riding through the Tetrarchate we had saddles . . . it's not exactly easy, you know.'

'Can't you use magic to make yourself a better rider?' he asked and she made a sound of irritation.

'I would think by now you'd have realized it doesn't work that way,' she said.

Alex smiled, since she couldn't see him. He had the beginnings of an idea as to how magic worked. But right now the important thing seemed to be to keep her talking. Since the twins were so susceptible to Verpertine's powers, Morgan's magic was the strongest weapon they had. He needed to keep her at least roughly oriented in the direction of sanity in case they had to call upon her powers again.

They rode out from the trees on to the shore of a wide flat lake, filled with some kind of viney water-plant that had crawled down from the opposite hillside. Looking up at the sharp crags opposite, silhouetted against the pearl-grey sky, Alex saw the round shape of a tower rising out of the rock.

'That's where we're going?' he asked.

The twins had already dismounted and were murmuring to each other, as they stood together on the shores of the lake. Following suit, Alex slid off the horse and turned to help catch Morgan as she awkwardly followed.

'It'll take too long to skirt the lake,' Charm said, as they approached. 'We should ford it and climb the crags ahead; the vines will provide some purchase.' She looked from Ciren to Alex and Morgan. 'Will you be able to manage?'

'I can,' Ciren said, still looking weak but determined, and Morgan said:

'I'll have to.'

Alex nodded, not intending to be outdone. But it surprised him when without another word Charm leapt out into the lake. She hadn't even attempted to take off her boots or protect her weapons but already she was forging ahead through the water, with a powerful crawl stroke. Ciren headed after her more circumspectly, wading in through the rushes at the edge. But within metres the water was up to his chest and he too began to swim, striking out for the opposite edge.

Alex considered for a moment before unlacing his boots and knotting them together. The twins might be able to swim in theirs but he didn't much fancy making the attempt, especially with all those strands of greenery floating beneath the water, reminding him uncomfortably of the grey web of Vespertine's spell. As an afterthought he dumped his leather tunic on the ground, abandoning it. Tying the boots with a simple knot to his sword belt he unbuckled the sword and held it in his right hand as he stepped into the lake. The water was cold but not chill. All the same it seeped through his clothes unpleasantly as he waded forward.

Behind him, Morgan had slid with difficulty down the muddy bank, hampered by the long skirt of her gown. But, once in the water, she managed an inelegant but effective swimming stroke, halfway between breast-stroke and doggy-paddle, passing him in the water. Her long black hair swirled around her face like the cloud of her magic and he wondered why it had manifested like that. Was it something intrinsic in the magic itself or a visualization of something in Morgan's mind?

Before long though, his own mind was occupied with the difficulties of swimming while holding the weight of the sabre. He'd always been a decent swimmer, certainly better than Morgan, if not up to the twins' standard. But his sword was more cumbersome than Charm's and it made it all but impossible to adopt any kind of swimming stroke. The mats of vegetation were a mixture of help and hindrance. They provided something to buoy up the weight of the sword but they tangled around his feet and legs so that he was always more floundering than swimming.

About halfway across the lake his arms began to ache and he thought more than once of giving up and letting the sword sink into the water. But without it he would be powerless once again and he had no idea of how difficult it would be to cross through this secret Door they were heading for. Tendrils clutched around his ankle and he swore to counteract fear. Each time it happened he felt certain it was Vespertine's spell catching up with them. Certainly the weeds seemed to display an almost human obstinacy, but they released him when he kicked free.

The tendrils got thicker towards the other side and it was possible to use them to pull himself through the water until he reached the first jutting spars of rock. The twins were waiting there, clinging to vines that covered the rock wall, and Morgan floated in the water near by. As Alex hauled himself out the twins started to move again, with fixed determination, making their way up the cliffside with ruthless efficiency. Alex waited for a moment, easing the aching muscles in his shoulders and trying to catch his breath for the climb.

Morgan gave him an odd look and then pulled herself

out of the water. Her hair was straggling over her shoulders and her blue silk gown clung slickly to her body. She flushed briefly as she saw him noticing, and then made a face.

'How the hell am I supposed to climb in this?' she asked, yanking at the long wet skirt with irritation. Pulling it up to knee height she tried to rip at the fabric and Alex moved over to help her.

'Here,' he said, managing to unsheath his sword and holding part of the skirt away from her legs so that he could snag it with the tip of the blade. Ripping through the heavy wet silk he managed to tear a long jagged slit from halfway down the skirt to the hem.

'Thanks,' Morgan muttered a bit brusquely, knotting the rest of the fabric up around her long bare legs for the climb.

He didn't blame her for feeling embarrassed. The gown was an even greater hindrance for what they were attempting than his heavy sabre.

Buckling the sword back around his waist beside his boots, he grabbed hold of the long snaking vines and began to climb. It wasn't unlike that slippery slope up through the middens of Shattershard as he and Jhezra had put into action their plot to take over the city. But at least this water was clean, he told himself, as he scraped and slid through the sharp rocks.

Looking up at Morgan eeling her way up the cliffside, he had to admit he was kind of impressed. It was one thing for Jhezra to have managed such a climb, she was a warrior and used to living in inhospitable conditions, but Morgan was just a schoolgirl, two years younger than he was, and she hadn't baulked at any part of their escape.

'Pretty incredible escape,' he said, grinning at her as his climb brought him up alongside Morgan.

'Not as incredible as Kal and me escaping Shattershard,' she said, meeting his eyes with a green glare that almost made him lose his grip on the slimy vine.

Alex winced and said nothing.

Laura looked out at the white world of Fenrisnacht as the Wolves loaded up the dog-sleighs. The snow had stopped falling and the settlement seemed busy with activity. She could glimpse the upright figures of people moving along the walkways and around the houses; there were smells of cooking meat and noises of ringing metal and clanking wood. And continually the surging bodies of the wolf-like dogs came and went around the traces of the sleighs.

Keeping to the side of the building she held herself apart from the mêlée and wondered at the deeper blur of blackness from the sky above. They'd been here for at least twelve hours, she was sure. Long enough at any rate for a new day to have dawned. But Jhezra had confirmed for her that the sky remained black overhead.

How hard would it be to find this place again, she wondered. Glossali Intergrade had taught her mnemonics to help her remember twists and turns of the Great Library despite her blindness. She thought perhaps she might be able to retrace Lisle's route from the Jurist section to the hidden Door they had used to arrive. But this world was so bleak and empty, she wondered how long someone might wait in that little roundhouse by the Door, before a border patrol discovered them.

*Perhaps not all that long.* She smiled as she remembered Kal's recommendation to the queen that she control the Doors, or risk others doing it instead. The Archon had learned from his experience, that was a point in his favour, even if it had led him to massively distrust her.

'I think we are nearly ready to leave,' a voice said near by and she recognized it as Jhezra's. Laura turned to look, and made out Zoë's red-brown head of curls spilling out of the hood of a cloaked figure behind her. Behind them Kal stood, wearing the white furs of Fenrisnacht as if he had been born to them.

'All right,' Laura said. Before long the darkness would close over her vision again and, preparing herself, she bound a scarf across her eyes. She remembered Lisle's warning of snow-blindness but in all truth she didn't want to prolong the pleasure of seeing, even indistinctly, when she knew she would lose it again. Nonetheless the bright white light could still be seen through the fabric as she made her way to the sleighs.

'What were you thinking?' Jhezra asked, in the gentle tones that meant she was pitying Laura again.

'About the darkness,' she said, thinking back to the last thoughts she was prepared to admit to, taking her seat in the sleigh Jhezra directed her to. 'The night-time sky . . . surely we've been here long enough for the sun to rise?'

'The night lasts long on Fenrisnacht,' she heard Lisle say, as the older woman joined them and the wriggling body of the dog called Pepper pushed its way past Laura's legs into the sleigh.

'You know, I was thinking,' Zoë said softly, joining them. 'It's probably snowing back home on Earth. At least it might be . . .' She paused and then added in a smaller voice: 'I think it must be nearly Christmas there.'

'Want to stop and decorate a fir tree?' Laura asked and felt Zoë stiffen up next to her.

'Actually,' Zoë said, moving away. 'I think I'll ride in the other sleigh with Jhezra and Kal.'

'Suit yourself,' Laura said, shrugging, and she could almost feel Lisle watching her as Zoë went quickly away.

There were a few final calls from the Wolves to each other and eager barking from the dogs and with a crack of a whip the sleigh jerked into motion. Feeling for one of the thick furs and pulling it over her knees Laura closed her eyes against the blurred light. Even then she could see it glowing pinkly through her eyelids.

'In Mandarel . . .' Lisle began to say and Laura lifted a hand to stop her.

'I'm very tired,' she said. 'And I'd like to rest. Will you tell me later?'

'As you prefer,' Lisle said, falling silent.

But although she didn't open her eyes Laura knew she wouldn't sleep, waiting for the inevitable and final blackness of the next Door.

As the round pillar of the tower loomed ahead Ciren could sense the Door inside the walls, enmeshed at the centre of another web of spells. From high up on the crag he turned to look back down the valley and his flesh chilled as he saw that a grey mist was lying heavily over the fields.

Mist typically settled, but this one was rising and he shuddered at the sight.

'We have no time to waste,' Charm said beside him, turning to look back for their companions. They came up over the lip of the cliff together. Morgan's dress was torn at the hip and it clung to her damply, smeared with green and brown stains from the wet and rotting vegetation they had climbed through. Ciren's clothes weren't in a much better state but he peeled off his black wool tunic and squeezed as much of the water as he could from it before offering it to Morgan. The air of the clifftop felt even colder through his thin shirt but he guessed she must be near frozen and her pale skin looked almost blue.

'Thank you,' she stammered through chattering teeth and Charm looked across at her with a strange expression in her eyes.

'Morgan will succumb to hypothermia if we do not make haste,' she said. 'And from the condition of the land below it seems Vespertine has remobilized his forces.'

'How are you planning to get past that then?' Alex asked, gesturing up at the tower. He had managed to retain his sword and one hand rested on it, ready for attack. 'I don't see a door. Of the magical kind or even a regular one.'

He was right, Ciren realized. The tower was perfectly round and made of smooth obsidian stone. There wasn't so much as a seam between building blocks to indicate where an entrance might be hidden.

'If our memories are intact, we came out of a Door here,' Charm said. 'But I can't recall how we exited.'

'Vespertine's spell caught us on the edge of the Door,' Ciren said. 'The tower is inside out, all the fortifications aimed inwards, it's a trap for anyone arriving from the other side.'

'That's not much of an answer,' Alex said with an edge of tension and Morgan picked up on it to add:

'The fog has reached the woods, we have to go . . .'

'Can we climb the tower?' Charm asked, her voice still level and apparently undaunted by the idea of a climb up a sheer wall if there were some way to do it.

'There may be a better way . . .' Ciren hesitated. He didn't much like the implications of his idea but it seemed possible it might work. 'The tower is made of the same black stone as our amulets, it's scattered in deposits through this world. I think perhaps there is some magic property in the obsidian and Vespertine's own magic channels its power.'

'I remember,' Morgan said, her eyes wide with wonder. 'You told me there was magic trapped. I felt it. My own spell set some of it free.'

'Can you do that again?' Charm asked, gesturing at the smooth round curve of the wall. 'Let the magic free and use it to open a way?'

'I don't know . . .' Morgan seemed to slump, her eyelids closing for a moment and showing the deep shadows like bruises under her eyes. 'I'll try,' she said, opening her eyes again and looking up at the tower with weary resignation. 'You guys, step back. I don't know what'll happen when I do.'

Alex moved back with alacrity and Ciren stepped back to stand next to his twin.

'Her magic is stronger than we ever imagined,' Charm said quietly, as Morgan composed herself. 'I wonder how that can be when she knows nothing of how to use it.'

'I wonder . . .' Ciren shook his head. 'I think there's nothing that I don't wonder about any more. But I wonder most what our true world is like . . . that's one memory that has not returned.'

'If Morgan is successful we will discover the answer soon enough,' Charm replied impassively.

The pinprick stars that pierced the sky from horizon to horizon were not the same as the bright wheels of light that had shone above Kal's own world. As the sleigh skimmed over the white hills and valleys of Fenrisnacht, Kal watched them and wondered at the change.

Avoiding the company of Laura had placed him in the same sleigh as Jhezra and Zoë. At first they had not tried to speak above the noise of their departure from the settlement. But once the noise of the humans and dogs had been blanketed by the vast distances, Jhezra spoke aloud:

'I have wondered if the black sky is like the blackness of the Doors. Perhaps each star is a world that can be travelled to.'

'Stars aren't worlds,' Zoë said, surprised into speech and then looking embarrassed when Kal and Jhezra turned towards her. 'I mean . . . they're like suns. Worlds are planets . . .' She must have seen their incomprehension because she shook her head and started again. 'I'm sorry. I'm not explaining it well. But stars can't be worlds, although they could have worlds surrounding them.'

'Each world is a sphere,' Kal said, taking up the explanation. 'While it appears that the sun moves around it from horizon to horizon, in fact it is the world that revolves about the sun. The suns of distant worlds are so far away they appear as small stars of light in the night sky.'

'This is not lore I have ever heard of,' Jhezra said, amazed. 'How do you know these things are so?'

'I learnt about it at school,' Zoë said, and her eyes travelled to Kal's face.

'I learnt . . .' Kal paused, trying to remember how he knew it. He was certain that what he had said was true but any memory of learning it was strangely absent. 'Morgan spoke once of the spheres,' he said in the end and the two girls dropped their eyes simultaneously.

He hadn't meant to make them feel guilty. But neither spoke for a while and his mind continued to fret at the question. *How had he known it?*

'Then what do you think the Doors might be?' Jhezra asked, intrigued. Kal looked for Zoë's answer and she shrugged, ruefully.

'I don't know. They're not something that people on my world know about. They're a bit like black holes. I suppose we'd call them a warp-hole in the space continuum, or something.' She laughed, awkwardly, and Jhezra looked completely mystified.

'I don't understand,' she said. 'The words don't seem to mean anything. What do you mean by the Door being in space when it is space that is in the Door?'

Now it was Zoë who looked blank and Kal frowned. All three of them wore translation amulets. Zoë's was of the type made in Shattershard and Jhezra's similar, his own Lisle's gift since he lacked the magic of his crown. But there seemed to be gaps in the translation, gaps that his memories were skipping over as smoothly as their sleigh slid across the white ice.

'Space is a word for the black void between stars,' he said. 'A black hole is a part of space that draws matter to it, as worlds and suns do each other. A Door is like a controlled black hole and a Gate . . .' He stopped abruptly.

'Go on . . .' Jhezra said. 'I understand it when you explain, I think. What is a Gate?'

Kal tipped his head back and stared up at the sky. His thoughts wheeled around and about each other like the stars in their courses. *How was it possible that he knew what he knew?*

'A Gate is a hole in space that opens far above the world. Larger than any Door could possibly be, they link worlds from star to star . . .'

'But how could you travel through such a thing?' Jhezra asked. 'To fall from such a height would kill you.'

'It sounds like a Door for spaceships,' Zoë said and Kal jerked upright, fixing his eyes on her.

'What did you say?' he demanded.

'Just that it sounded as if it might be meant for spaceships . . .' Zoë said, looking almost frightened. 'You wouldn't have heard of them. They're not real anyway.'

'But they are.' Kal tried to comprehend the ramifications of his own words.

The conversation was opening up new vistas of knowledge inside his brain, almost too great for him to bear. 'Ships that sail through space and travel from Gate to Gate as we do Doors.'

'Is it a kind of magic?' Jhezra asked, turning her own gaze upwards. 'Are they flying up there now?'

'It's not possible,' Zoë said, her faced pinched with a tight frown. 'You couldn't do that with magic . . . surely?'

'It's possible,' Kal said. 'I don't know how but I know it's so. In my dreams I've seen them fly. And fall.'

He shuddered, clenching his hands and feeling the sting of the cuts the surgeon had bandaged. In his pack he carried the object that had left those marks, the mesh of thorny spikes that he knew as the Archon's crown. He'd kept it with him, though he dared not wear it, and it seemed he could feel its presence, waiting for him to lift it to his head once more. The marks it had left on him were more than those hairline cuts across his fingers, it was the knowledge locked behind doors in his head he feared.

'Forgive me,' he murmured. 'I'm not myself.' And even as the others nodded their understanding he wondered what he meant.

Morgan shivered convulsively in her sodden clothes. She felt small and insignificant beside the black tower. Alex looked dead tired, still clutching the hilt of his sword for comfort and even the twins seemed pale and washed out next to the black wall of stone.

Amulets made of the same stone had circled the twins'

necks, like collars keeping them on Vespertine's leash. This tower was like a massive shackle around the Door Ciren had insisted was there. Morgan's magic felt weak and feeble compared to the power she could sense pulsing through the black stone. Staring at it she wondered if she could really see the grey veins marbling the obsidian or if she only feared she did. Extending her hands towards the tower in a gesture of appeal she reached for the magic.

It flowed into her mind like the black wine of Shattershard, soothing her fears and warming her with reassurance. It was hers to take and use, more so than Vespertine's. He had trapped it in his orderly web but what it wanted was to be free. She could smash the tower in splinters if she chose, or cleave it in two like butter. Instead she let the power spill out of her like liquid heat and saw the black stone bubble and melt like candle wax, opening a path inside.

'Go, Morgan,' Alex cheered. But as he and the twins closed up the gap between them, they saw what she had seen. Through the gap another wall of tower was visible, curving off to either side, a wall within the wall.

'I remember this,' Ciren murmured. 'The fortifications are concentric circles, like ripples in a lake.'

Morgan stepped into the empty gap in the walls, and concentrated. Again the magic splashed out of her into the stone, melting another hole in the wall. The next circle was lower down and she stumbled as she stepped through the gap. Alex reached to catch her arm and she didn't object. She raised only her right hand to gesture at the next wall and they all watched as the rock withered back slowly.

'I'm tired,' Morgan said and Alex squeezed her arm.

'You're doing great,' he told her. 'Not far now.'

There was no way he could know that but his show

of concern did comfort her and as they moved on in fits and starts, each wall taking longer to melt, Morgan leant more and more heavily on his supporting arm.

The magic was as strong as ever but her mind was getting tired. It was dark inside the tower and her eyelids felt heavy, dragged down by the irresistible urge to sleep. It was a shock when she raised her hand and Alex pulled her back.

'Watch out,' he said and two voices said in unison:

'The Door.'

The blackness in front of her lacked the sheen of the obsidian or the private warmth of her shut eyes. It was the absolute darkness that signalled a Door. They stood at the entrance and Morgan tried as always to look through it to the other side but it was impossible.

'Are we sure this is a good idea?' she asked. Now that it came to it, Morgan felt assailed by doubt. At least they knew what to expect of the Library, even if it was under the Wheel's control. All they knew about this Door was that Vespertine had locked it. How could they be sure that they would find allies on the other side?

'We can't know that,' Charm said.

'We can only trust,' Ciren echoed.

'I think it's what they call a leap of faith,' Alex added. 'Besides, how can it possibly be worse than what we've been through already?'

Famous last words, Morgan thought. But she said nothing. It was too late to turn back now. Taking a deep breath she stepped forward and entered the Door.

Zoë had been expecting another roundhouse but the sleighs came to a halt halfway up the slope of a hill. The Wolf warriors' faces had the studied indifference of soldiers who've been told not to question their destination and Zoë remembered another similar incident with the Hajhim back in Shattershard.

'We're here,' Lisle called, stepping out on to the snow, her dog bounding out after her.

Zoë looked up the hill but she saw nothing. No round-house, not so much as a circle of stones to mark where a Door might be.

'Is it under the snow?' she asked dubiously.

'It's straight ahead,' Lisle said with a smile. 'At the top of the hill. But it's near impossible to see.'

Kal and Jhezra joined Zoë in looking upwards, trying to glimpse it, as Lisle turned to say farewell to the Wolves. Laura stood a little apart from them all, the scarf wrapped across her face like a flag of challenge that Zoë had no idea how to respond to.

They waited until the sleighs left, the dogs barking as they were whipped up again into motion and their yipping barks ringing out across the snow as they disappeared with surprising speed to become only dots in the distance.

'Shall we go,' Lisle said, setting the pace uphill.

Jhezra moved to help Laura, and Zoë started off before it would look as if she was waiting for Kal to help her as well.

'I think I see it,' Jhezra said as they came up over the crest of the hill. She raised a hand and Zoë looked where she pointed.

It was a patch of blackness, a starless place in the sky. Its position on the top of the hill had hidden it until they were right up next to it and as Zoë finally realized that it was a Door her thoughts flew to Kal's strange remarks about Gates. Suddenly that didn't seem so impossible after all.

'Someone said science is like magic, to people who don't understand it,' she said quietly, not sure which of the others she was talking to. 'Does that mean that magic could be a science, if you could understand how it worked?'

'My world has never had much of either,' Lisle replied. 'It was strange to discover a world like Mandarel which had so much of each. Perhaps there you'll find your answer.'

'Or more questions,' Kal replied.